David Tudor grew up in North Yorkshire and now lives in London. *Swank* is his first book.

DAVID TUDOR

Swank

PALADIN
GRAFTON BOOKS
A Division of the Collins Publishing Group

LONDON GLASGOW
TORONTO SYDNEY AUCKLAND

Paladin
Grafton Books
A Division of the Collins Publishing Group
8 Grafton Street, London W1X 3LA

Published in Paladin Books 1987

First published in Great Britain by
Jonathan Cape Ltd 1985

ISBN 0-586-08599-8

Printed and bound in Great Britain by
Collins, Glasgow

Set in Palatino

To Liz, with thanks

CONTENTS

LIFE

The light was very bright and the talking and the music were very loud and everyone was smiling and relaxed and enjoying themselves.

John was getting very drunk. He was starting to look for flies, looking under the sofa and the chairs, looking under the chaos of bottles on the table.

'Have you got any flies on you?' he asked Marion, trying to look down the top of her shirt because she wasn't wearing a bra.

A fly obligingly appeared on the table, and with surprising deftness John brought his hand down neatly over the top of it. He teased it into place between his fingers, then picked it up, tore off its wings, and popped it in his mouth.

He pretended to chew it. Paul pretended to be sick.

They forgot about John for a while and the conversation turned to music. Ellen, a Patti Smith fan, was talking with great animation until, just about to take some more Guinness, she stopped with the bottle halfway to her mouth and stared at John, feeling nauseous.

Everyone else stopped what they were doing and stared too. The fly was painfully crawling its way out of John's left nostril. John was delighted with their reaction. He caught hold of the fly and put it back in his mouth. This time he really did chew it and swallow it.

'Oh Christ,' someone said.

'I once knew a kid who used to eat spiders,' lied Rick. 'This was in the third year, before I came up here. Once he got a whole load of spiders in a box and took them into class. He sat down, put all the spiders in his mouth, and tapped the girl in front of him on the shoulder. When she turned round he opened his mouth slightly and all the spiders began to crawl out. She threw up.'

'Did you see on telly that thing about New York where there was a march by the American Nazis?' Kathy volunteered. 'It wasn't like the NF marches. They had boots and helmets and armbands and flags with swastikas on them.'

'They're idiots,' said someone.

'There were people watching who said they agreed with them.'

'The blacks and the Jews,' said Julie.

'Like that whatsit,' said Rick, 'the Klu Klux Klan.'

'And they were giving out pamphlets listing all Begin's crimes as a terrorist.'

'That's right,' put in Paul. 'Begin was a terrorist, just like Arafat.'

'The Jews were the ones who wrecked any chance of peace in the Middle East,' said John. 'It was all those rich Jewish financiers who blackmailed the British and the Americans into creating Israel in the first place.'

'Well they do have a right to their homeland,' said Kathy.

'So do the Palestinians,' said Paul.

The night wore on. Around 12.30 a.m. John and Rick wandered out on to the balcony of the flat. John finished off his lager and threw the bottle as far out as he could. It landed with a crash on the other side of the street. He went back inside and grabbed up all the empty bottles he could carry and took them on to the balcony. The others began to drift after him to see what he was up to.

'Watch me hit that building,' he said, and lobbed a bottle at the block across the street. It fell only a few feet short, and smashed eight floors down on the pavement.

'That's no good,' said Rick. He picked up a bottle and threw it. It too fell short. Willing hands launched three more bottles, all unsuccessfully.

'Hold it, there's somebody down there,' someone said.

They watched in silence as a man walked two-thirds of the way down the street on the other side of the road.

'Watch this,' said John, and threw a bottle. It was a good shot, and smashed only a few feet behind its target.

The man started and looked back, then looked up thinking it had come from the building beside him. He walked quickly out of sight.

Another man appeared, this time on their side of the road.

'Look at that guy,' said Rick. 'He looks like he's gay.'

'How do you know he's gay?' said Marion.

'I dunno. He just looks like one.'

John got ready to throw a bottle. 'Hey, no, wait,' said Rick. 'I'll be right back.'

He went back inside and returned a minute later with a full bottle.

'Don't waste the beer,' said Marion.

'It's only water,' said Rick.

Rick held the bottle upright at arm's length over the edge of the balcony. Everyone held their breath and suppressed their giggles in case the man should look up. But he walked on unsuspecting. When he was almost right under them Rick let the bottle drop.

It crashed down just in front of him, showering him with glass and water. They rushed back inside and lay laughing helplessly.

John ran back out to see the man hurrying away.

Rick joined him.

'Fucking fag!' shouted Rick.

'Hey, fag!' shouted John.

'Has he gone?' asked Marion.

The rest reappeared, and after a while another bottle was thrown at the block across the street. The next one was a direct hit and went crashing through a window.

'Oh shit,' said John, and they fled back inside.

'Somebody's going to call the police,' said Ellen.

'We were only having fun,' said Rick, quite seriously, then exploded into laughter.

John began spraying him with cider.

'Hey, watch the carpet,' said Marion.

Julie closed the bedroom door behind her and shut her eyes. The room was in semi-darkness. Behind her eyelids it was deep black. She hugged her arms around herself. Her brow was furrowed.

'Julie?'

Her eyes started open. What was I doing? she thought, wildly.

Someone was lying on the bed, head turned towards her. It was Jennifer. She could make out the long blonde hair and the cheap white dress. She crossed over to the window and sat on the sill, looking back into the room. She felt ill at ease, as if discovered in the midst of some grim secret.

Jennifer spoke first.

'Do you ever have dreams?'

Julie said nothing.

'Do you think it means anything if you die in your dreams?'

Julie wanted to rub her hand over her forehead and her eyes, to try and rub away the aching. 'No,' she said. 'Not really.' What is she doing here? Go away.

'I had this really strange dream last night. I was in a car, and the car was fastened to a big balloon, and it kept bobbing about in the wind. But the balloon wasn't light enough and I was only a couple of feet off the ground. And I kept drifting on to the road and other cars kept smashing into me.' She thought for a moment. 'I remember it was sunny. Really sunny.'

Julie felt a sudden qualm of anxiety. She'd got a job in a big shop, and through having a job she had got a flat, and now her supervisor was giving her trouble about coming in late and not looking interested. If the job went everything else would go with it.

'I don't suppose it means anything,' she said to Jennifer.

'Once in a dream I fell down a stairwell. I was holding on by one hand, but my fingers hurt and I couldn't keep my grip, and I was really scared because I was going to die and I felt so helpless. And then I lost my grip altogether and I was terrified as I fell, but I never hit the bottom. Isn't that strange?'

'Yeh.' There was laughter coming from the party. There was a golden sliver of light beneath the door, and now she was becoming accustomed to the darkness she could make out, without really being aware or interested in it, the faint crack of light around the sides and top of the door as well. 'I suppose I'd better get back,' she said. Go away. My head aches.

'Another time I drowned,' said Jennifer, 'I tried to breathe, and all I got in my lungs was water. I couldn't even choke. I just flailed my arms about, trying to get above the surface. I've never been so scared. Do you ever have dreams like that?'

Julie remembered watching her funeral, the blue-black sky, the torches, the hooded figures, the casket. She shuddered. 'No,' she said.

'I do,' said Jennifer. 'All the time.'

Julie blinked at the too bright light in the bathroom. She closed the door and leaned heavily on the washbasin.

She stared at herself in the mirror. She looked tired, pinched. Her eyes were dark pools of exhaustion. All her emotions had sunk to the pit of her stomach, into a bottomless depression. It was an old, very familiar depression. Just those few words of Jennifer's were enough to set off a too familiar train of thought.

Death.

I want to die.

Not, she felt, a great tragedy, just a simple fact. She did not even know why, although she could probably invent enough false reasons if she thought about it for a while.

She ran the nail of her right index finger over her left wrist. Then, cautiously, she scratched hard enough to scrape the skin slightly. It didn't hurt. She looked around. There was a razor, she could use that.

She took out the blade and ran it experimentally across her wrist. Her arm tingled with apprehension.

She imagined slashing right through her wrist, through the skin, the flesh, the nerves, the muscle, right through to the bone. Her stomach lurched and she leaned back against the wall feeling faint.

'Coward,' she whispered.

She put back the razor and ran her hands under the cold water, then rubbed the water over her forehead. As she dried, the thoughts kept repeating themselves, around and around and around in her head. Someday. One day.

She brushed back her hair, touched up her make-up, straightened out her clothes, and went back to the party.

THE VICTIM

We first saw this guy in the room at the back of the hall where the bands all were. He was straight looking, not middle class slumming straight, but the hangdog miserable type, the not-too-bright misfit who was so gawky and ill put together that he always got left out and was always the butt of the crudest jokes.

He shouldn't have been back there at all. He'd come round to put on this weird costume he hadn't the nerve to wear on the street. He'd seen all the pictures in the papers, and so he'd brought a girl's stocking to put over his head, black plastic rubbish bags for shirt and trousers, a long necklace of safety pins, and a fedora.

His aim was the big social splash, the twin rewards of friendship and appreciation through looking good and acting cool. God knows why he'd come looking for them here. The friendship and appreciation of dedicated bachelor ramblers would probably have been closer to his natural style.

I remember Paul went up and talked to him for a while, but otherwise we all ignored him.

We should have booted the poor sod out right there.

The first band starts playing, and I go out to the front during the second song, and there is this same arsehole dancing about by himself and really going crazy. All askew and messy. Looking the complete idiot.

And of course, once he's started he has to keep it up. Putting on a show and doesn't know how to stop.

You get them like that. I once saw this bloke who invented a new dance. What he would do is run about the hall like some kind of fucking jogger. And of course, again, once he'd started he thought he was on show and everyone was watching him, and he didn't know how to stop. So there he was, running around half the night as if he'd lost his memory on his way to the marathon.

And a right clown he looked, as well.

Same with this kid.

In some ways it was good. People here are usually slow at starting to dance, but he got them moving right away. Those who wanted to dance but didn't want to be the first to start felt safe from too much attention with this lunatic throwing himself about. So things got hopping quite quickly that night.

Early on, the kid's hat comes off. So Derek happens to be walking across the hall and he kicks it out of the way, then someone else kicks it down the back stairs, and as far as I know he never did get his hat back.

Then John wades in there. There's still only a few people dancing, so John's sort of putting on a show too.

Except his show is to cut the kid up. He rips off the plastic bags one by one, and the guy's laughing, grinning away, thinking someone's joining in the fun with him. Of course, he's getting all these negative vibes off John, can't help but do so, but he's too stupid to realise he's being dumped on, and he laughs away while John rips up his costume.

Then John starts knocking him about a bit. Not hard, you understand, just starting a little punching, roughing him up a bit. And the kid still wants to think it's all a joke and all good fun, and so he's grinning away while John's punching him and throwing him about the floor.

And finally John just gives up. I mean, you can see his point. What do you do with someone like that?

So anyway, the kid would have got off fairly lightly if he hadn't been such a fucking glutton for punishment.

At the end of the evening he's still hanging around and trying to come on all friendly with the bands, trying to show everyone else that he's in and knows all the right people.

All the bands and their friends are going off to a party, so Rick invites this arsehole along, just for a laugh. And the arsehole's preening himself and thinking he's so cool and such a fucking hit.

So we all go to the party, and once there Rick hops up on this wide sill on this window high up in the wall. And then John grabs his legs and tries to pull him down, but he can't. So John gets up there too.

The arsehole is sitting on the couch just below them. Rick and John have got this bowl of boiled sweets up there, and the berk is wanting a sweet but they won't let him have any.

Finally he gives up and so, not yet tired of him, they start pelting him with them. You know: 'Hey, here's a sweet!' Kapow! 'Hey, d'you want another?' Zap!

And the arsehole's going, 'Fuck off!' and getting all annoyed, and so Rick and John just enjoy it all the more, and just keep throwing sweets at him until they're all gone.

Then Rick starts pouring lager on the guy's head.

That's pretty funny. He doesn't like that at all. But instead of just moving out of the way he gets all angry again, and keeps telling Rick to fuck off. So Rick starts kicking him as well, and John pours some gin over his head.

Then things quieten down for a while, but later John and Rick are sitting on the couch and the arsehole is on the floor listening to the music, and they keep pushing him with their feet. The idiot thinks it wouldn't be manly to get out of the way, so he stays where he is. John and Rick think this is pretty funny in such a dink, so they kick him a little harder.

Finally John says, quietly, to Rick, 'Let's throw him in the bath.'

So they try to pick him up, and he struggles a bit, but doesn't really know what's going on until John says, 'We're going to give you a bath,' and then he flails about and shouts, 'No way,' and 'Fuck off,' and we all join in and get him dragged halfway down the corridor, but eventually give up. Too much trouble, you know, with him kicking away like some kind of fucking girl.

So then we leave him alone for a while.

Later on someone calls him a faggot, for no particular reason, just to see what he would do.

And wouldn't you know, he gets angry all over again and starts telling everyone to fuck off (what a vocabulary!) and shouting, 'I'm not a queer!'

And he's sitting beside Rick, and Rick's calling him a fag, too, so he starts hitting Rick and trying to beat him up.

Of course, it might as well be a three year old attacking Rick. And Rick's treating the whole thing as if it were some kind of homo assault, and saying things like, 'You're so beautiful when you're angry,' and 'Kiss me, kiss me,' and everyone's laughing and the berk's getting more and more pissed off.

And eventually he gets fed up, announces he's leaving, and walks out.

And good riddance.

So the party goes on for quite a while, and everyone has a good time with good loud music on the stereo and good people and good booze, a really good time.

Anyway, we're just leaving around 2.30 a.m., and who should turn up at the front door but this same arsehole. Seems he thinks he might be missing something, and has come back for more. He's even got himself a bottle of vodka from somewhere, no doubt to prove he's a man and can drink the hard stuff.

So we let him walk down the street with us, but before long he's getting all jokey and chummy, and starts throwing vodka all over Derek. So Derek roughs him up, and then he's a bit quieter, although he's still tagging along.

And so Rick says, 'Why don't you smash in that car window?' and of course the fool, thinking this must be how he's supposed to act, picks up a largish rock and, with a lot of effort, succeeds in making a hole in the car windscreen. Of course, we don't want to know about it, and we don't want him with us in case anyone saw. But he follows along and, as it seems no one did see, we begin to take a little more notice of him.

He just preens himself under the attention, thinks he's accepted and part of the crowd and all that, and tries to get fresh with Swank's girlfriend.

So Swank smashes him in the mouth and makes his lip bleed.

The dink looks sort of rueful, but cheers up when he hears Derek say, 'Oh, leave him alone,' and assumes everything's all right again.

A short while later Rick spots this old tyre lying by the road, and proceeds to kick it about. The arsehole joins in, but instead of kicking the tyre he keeps bumping into Rick, thinking he's going to prove himself a man by getting even with the bastard who stole his sweets from him.

So Rick thumps him a few times.

We're all standing around watching and laughing, and the creep starts getting all annoyed and upset and starts wanting a real fight. And so Rick thumps him some more, then turns away, not really wanting to beat the little wimp up.

But this kid's a really hopeless case, you know. I mean, he doesn't know when people are being nice to him.

Rick turns his back, and the kid jumps on him and tries to beat him up. It's pretty pathetic, and what else can Rick do except shake him off and thump him a couple more times?

But the arsehole won't leave well enough alone. He gives this stupid cry of rage and throws himself at Rick, clawing and flailing his arms about like some adolescent female.

So Rick really gives it to him, really knocks him about.

He's a hell of a lot quieter after that, but he's still tagging along and saying things like, 'Why did you do that?' and 'Don't you like me?' and 'Are you trying to get even with me for something?'

And everyone's saying, 'Fuck off' and 'Get lost' and 'Go to hell', but the little prick keeps tagging along, trying to make out like he's still one of the group and this is some kind of internal squabble and he's been roughed up quite wrongly.

So then John has a go at him, and has him down on the grass and is punching him in the face until Kevin drags him off.

'Now fuck off,' said Rick.

But the shithead keeps hanging around.

I mean, this is the kind of creep who just sits there and begs to get his fucking head kicked in.

So Rick gives him a few kicks, although not in the head. And we're all getting pretty pissed off by now, and this is getting to be a *real* drag, so everyone takes a couple of kicks at him. Then Rick gives him a push from behind and at the same time Swank kicks him, pow! right in the face. And Swank's wearing hard boots. He splits the creep's mouth right open and there's blood pouring all over the ground.

John gives him a kick in the side of the head and Rick gives him another good push, and he rolls over and lies in the dust.

He's holding his head and swearing at us. So we hit him some more.

We finally get tired of this. It's sort of like hitting a piece of cardboard, you know, gets a little dull.

But as we start to walk away, the arsehole recovers enough to get to his knees and start yelling all these obscenities at us.

It must have been the vodka. I mean, the dink was far too much of a wimp to get defiant like that without the unaccustomed stimulation.

So Rick picks up this big lump of wood, and he and John are just going to finish him off when these guys out joy riding in a car come speeding around the corner and run him over.

They killed him, of course.

And we scattered like fucking sparrows. Scared shitless. But we never got caught.

We didn't want it to happen to him. He was just some arsehole.

Fucking served him right, though.

SWANK

Swank said, 'What you need in this world is a good big dose of anaesthetic. Or else you need pills or booze. And if you don't have these things you try to anaesthetise yourself by putting on the stereo or watching TV or even reading a book. And the best thing to listen to is a good bit of violent, angry noise that gets it all out of your system, and even if you feel just as screwed up and angry afterwards at least you feel better for having expressed it in some way. The best books are the ones where the characters are strong enough and addictive enough that they take you away from what's outside you and allow you to connect with whatever there is inside – which usually isn't much. And the best TV shows are the ones that don't make you think.'

'There's never anything on TV anyway,' said Tony. 'I watch it all the time and there's never anything worth watching.'

'All that stuff about entertainment as a drug, as if it were all some sort of vicious plot, all that's crap. People want to be numbed, to be switched off. How else is the world bearable?'

'That's right. All you need is a good bit of half-hidden sex,' said Tony. 'Give me "Charlie's Angels" over "Panorama" any day. Although I used to watch the news when they had Anna Ford doing it.'

'What really gets me is that there's no way to hit back. No way at all. What do you do? Throw a bomb? Big deal. Twenty seconds on "News at Ten", then nothing. They understand throwing bombs, it's something they can deal with. They have laws to bureaucratise it, they can file you away and forget about it. It's their game, they wrote all the rules, you just play into their hands. Unless you get organised, in which case you just play into the hands of some paranoid thug with a political theory. So what do you do? Kill yourself? For what? Who'll care? Even your best friends will have forgotten you in a couple of months.'

'Yeh,' said Tony. 'I wouldn't mind putting a bomb under a couple of TV directors myself.'

'Swank, it's him,' said Carrie, taking him by the arm and pointing across to the other side of the room. 'That man at the club.'

Swank and Carrie had gone to a local night club a week before to hear Carrie's friend, Alison, make her singing début. It was a desiccated, middle-aged place that seldom got worthwhile talent any more, from London or anywhere else, and usually relied on local nonentities. But it was open late, and so was much frequented by the respectable drunks who turned up around midnight, already having difficulty walking up the stairs.

They arrived well in time for the first set. The host, a little man with slicked-back hair and neatly trimmed moustache, had stared at them, their ill attire, their boots, their trousers, their shabby leather jackets, Swank's short-cropped, severe black hair, Carrie's blonde shock, all without comment, while Carrie looked idly about her and Swank stared insolently back at him.

He led them silently to a table at the very back of the club, where the darkness was deepest. The rest of the club was almost empty.

'Who the fuck does he think he is?' Swank scowled, almost as soon as they sat down. Carrie pulled him back into his seat, anxious not to be thrown out altogether.

'Let's just move over there,' she said. They got up and crossed to a well-lit table close to the stage. None of the staff paid them any attention. But Swank stared hard at the host, and they both knew they would remember him if they ever saw him again.

'What's he doing here?' hissed Carrie. His well-cut suit and his over-gallant smile grated on her earthy sensibilities. She disliked him instinctively.

'Must have been invited by Alison,' said Swank.

'Well do something about it,' she whispered savagely. Then

she checked him as he moved towards the man. 'But don't cause any trouble.'

Swank leered at her.

The man started when he recognised Swank, but he put a good face on it. 'Hello,' he said, offering his hand. 'Didn't I see you once at the club?'

Swank took him by the arm and, making friendly talk, quietly manœuvred him away from the party and out into the corridor of the flat. The man looked apprehensive, licking his lips, pulling down the cuffs of his jacket, eyeing the sheathed knife Swank always wore at his belt, but still making a show of being amiable.

Swank leaned one arm against the wall and stared at him.

'Can you spare a quid?' he asked, keeping his voice friendly.

Uncertainty and relief alternated in the man's eyes. 'Yes, I think so,' he said. He took his wallet from his inside jacket pocket, took out a note, and handed it to Swank.

Swank put the money in his back pocket, but otherwise didn't move. The man stirred, ill at ease. He ran his fingers down the front of his jacket, as if wiping something off.

'How about five?' asked Swank, his voice neutral.

The man paused, and tried to look past Swank to see if there was anyone he could perhaps signal to. He managed a brief smile. 'Well. All right. If you really need it. Always glad to help out.' He handed over a fiver.

Swank took it. 'How about ten?' he asked.

'Look,' the man stammered. 'I really don't think this is, I mean, I can't stay here all night, you know.'

Swank took the wallet out of his hands and looked inside. There were two tens, another five, and several ones. He took the tens and the five, and gave back the wallet.

'Thanks, chief,' he said.

He rejoined Carrie and began ushering her out of the flat, grabbing their jackets on the way, calling out goodbyes.

'What did you do to him?' asked Carrie, once they were outside.

'Just borrowed a little drinking money,' said Swank, producing the notes.

'Great', Carrie grinned. She took the money and put it safely in her purse. 'Where are we going to drink it?'

They decided they would drink it at home, and piled up packs of Guinness in the back seat of the old car they had picked up. Swank drove while Carrie rolled some joints. They didn't talk much.

Carrie stared through the rain, and wondered which way they were going.

'You'll see,' said Swank.

He drove deliberately into the 'better' area of the city, where the houses were bigger and the streets were cleaner and the air was softer. After negotiating several winding suburban avenues, he stopped outside a large stylish house, three floors, thirties-Elizabethan, two-car garage, and a huge front lawn with a hedge to keep off dogs and people.

'That's where he lives,' said Swank.

Carrie was mystified. 'Who?' she asked.

'Boorman. Of Boorman's Galleries.'

'The one who turned down your paintings?'

Swank nodded.

'Creep,' she said.

On an impulse she rolled down the car window. 'Ya Creep!' she yelled, into the damp.

She rolled up the window and they both stared morosely at the house.

'Looks like he does all right for himself,' she observed.

'He's an over-educated arsehole,' said Swank. 'All he knows is prices and saleability and what they stuffed into him at university. He knows what a painting's worth, but he's no idea of what it's about.'

'Yeh, well just wait. You'll show him.'

'I'd like to fucking show him something now.'

Carrie laughed. 'A brick through the window.'

'A match to the hedge.'

'Obscene slogans on his front door.'

'Dirty phone calls to his wife.'

'Cut down his trees.'

'Blow up his car.'

Silence for a while.

'Come on, honey, let's go,' Carrie said, beginning to roll another joint. 'We don't need shitheads like that.'

Swank and Carrie had a flat on the second floor of an old

house, tall and narrow, converted like most of its brethren into flats and bedsits. Fire instructions had been pasted up inside the front door, and thick, heavy fire doors were at the top of each flight of stairs.

Their flat was two rooms, a dowdy living-room that also served as a kitchen, and an unkempt bedroom that doubled as a studio.

They took the booze into bed with them, the warmest place. They alternated snatches of half-interested love making with drinking and fragments of conversation. After a while it seemed as if time had become confused and perhaps they had been there for ever and it must surely be nearly morning. This one room with its yellow light and its familiar mess, it became their universe, time capsule, secure and secret refuge.

'I was talking to Ron today,' Carrie said. 'He said some bloke tried to rape Ellen.'

'I thought you weren't speaking to Ellen,' said Swank, after a while.

'No, Ron. I was talking to Ron.'

'Oh.' Swank lay with his eyes closed, irritated a little by the brightness of the light, wondering if he should switch it off.

'Anyway, why aren't you talking to Ellen?' he asked.

'Well, she said those things about you, didn't she? The cow.'

'Oh yeh,' said Swank. 'I'd forgotten.'

'Swank,' she said, some time later, 'Swank, what would you do if someone tried to attack me?'

'I dunno,' said Swank, sleepily. 'Let them, I suppose.'

'You bastard!' she cried, yanking the pillow from beneath his head and pounding him with it. 'That's not what you said when that guy at that party on Ellice Road got at me. There wasn't much of him left to tell about it.'

'Yeh, well . . .' Swank smiled, uncertain. He looked proud, pleased she had remembered. 'Can't have people cutting up my Carrie, can I?'

The night slipped by. There was a noise outside the window, someone throwing up down below. Carrie pulled a face. The door banged in the flat above them, and someone walked around for a few minutes in hard-heeled shoes on the wooden floor. Swank fumbled for a while with the rest of Carrie's clothes, but gave up before she was naked. They finished off another pack.

'This is the last of them,' said Swank, when he eventually found the energy to open up the final box. He sat on the bed and looked at her: messy, warm, and oddly sensuous. She told him to pass her a bottle.

'Watch this,' he said. He picked up an empty bottle by the neck and, turning his head away, slammed it down hard on the edge of the bedside cabinet. Fragments of glass flew about the room. The wooden cabinet sustained a large dent.

'Not bad, huh?'

He looked for a sharp edge on the broken neck and began to draw it slowly up his arm, leaving a thin red trail on the pale skin.

Carrie tried to look away, but couldn't. It did not seem to bother Swank, but she could feel the glass ripping through the skin every inch of the way. 'Stop it, Swank,' she pleaded.

He stopped when he reached his shoulder, and threw the neck into a corner. He put two fingers to the cut, then to his mouth, licking off the blood. 'Want some?' he asked, offering his arm.

'What do you do things like that for?' she said, pushing him away. 'You'll kill yourself, one day.'

'Yeh, well. No one's going to worry much about that, are they?'

'I would,' she said.

He stared at her for a few moments, then leaned over and kissed her.

'Sorry,' he said. 'I forgot.'

'Give me a drink.' He opened a bottle for her, then lay back down beside her.

They were silent. Carrie was remembering a drunken dare, with Swank deciding to sign his name in blood and taking a meat knife to his wrist to do so. At the hospital the doctor had looked piercingly at a recent bruise that her make-up only partially hid, and had asked her difficult questions.

It was like that woman cop at the station when Swank had been accused of stealing a car. She had been taken quietly aside and advised that Swank was not a good person to be around and she would be better off with someone more 'adjusted'.

'The bitch,' she muttered.

Swank grunted. He had forgotten his drink, and seemed to be asleep.

Then there was the time he had taken all those amphetamines, God knows how many he'd taken, dozens it seemed. He'd just kept taking them and taking them, more and more, because he was so depressed, he'd said, and wanted to OD. But he hadn't. Instead the depression and the pills had come together like oil and fire and he had knifed someone so badly outside a pub he felt sure he was going to be had up for murder and spent a whole week hiding, afraid to answer the door.

She smiled to herself. He was all right, was Swank. She often thought, half-tenderly, that for all his bravado he seemed quite incapable of looking after himself without her. And as for herself, until she had hooked up with him she had done nothing but slew about wildly from one fuck-up to the next. They needed each other. With very little exaggeration, they were all they really had.

Swank, apparently, was not asleep, for he sat up suddenly to get another bottle, quite forgetting the half empty one on the floor beside him.

He sat back against the wall, looking down on her, and took a swallow of his drink.

'Whore,' he said, following some line of thought of his own.

Carrie flinched. 'Don't call me that,' she said uneasily. She didn't like it when he got into those moods, with that cynical leer on his face.

'Well you were, weren't you,' he said. 'Whore.'

'Not for long I wasn't. And I'm not now. Besides,' she added defensively, 'nothing wrong with it.'

'Didn't say there was, did I?' said Swank. 'Whore.'

'Well what are you going on about it for?' she demanded. 'Leave me alone.'

'It's just I get tired of screwing a fucking Underground tunnel.'

Her face scrunched up with anger. She reached out impulsively for his knife on the cabinet and swung at him, leaving a neat gash on his left cheek, which bled slowly.

'Fucking cunt.' He grabbed her by the shoulder and delivered a sharp blow to her face, closing one eye.

After a while it became clear the eye was going to blacken.

He touched it gingerly with his fingertips. 'Does it hurt?' he asked, solicitously.

'Ouch, yes.' She got up to look in the mirror.

'Do you want me to get you something for it?'

She did not answer. 'Shit,' she said. 'Now I'm going to have to wear dark glasses till it goes away.' She climbed back on to the bed. 'And you're going to have to do something about that cut on your cheek.'

Swank shrugged. 'A bunch of toughs beat me up,' he said.

'Oh yeh. And that's nothing to what you did to them, right?'

'Right,' said Swank, and she rolled over on top of him, laughing.

An hour before dawn Swank found himself awake again. The light was hurting his eyes and he had a headache. He leaned painfully over to switch off the lamp, then lay back, sighing.

He was still smashed, his head still felt light, but his body felt empty, like a shell. He rooted cynically around for his heart and could not find it. There was nothing. All he felt was fucked up.

He looked over at Carrie. She was asleep, breathing gently through her partially opened mouth.

He felt suddenly too restless and too bitter to lie awake, so he got up, carefully, the sudden clanging in his head quietening down after he had stood still a while.

'Oh fuck,' he muttered.

Both hands holding his head, he staggered out into the other room. He reached a chair and fell into it, head lolling back, refusing to think.

He sat there a long while, the bitterness welling up, filling the emptiness.

'Bastards,' his mouth said, unbidden. He sat up suddenly and switched on the light. His paintings, or some of them, were laid untidily and temporarily against the wall.

They were rubbish. All of them, each of them, every one of them. Rubbish. What was he doing trekking about making a fool of himself with pathetic rubbish like this? Fucking rubbish.

'Swank?'

He did not want to talk to anyone. Not even her.

'Okay,' he called back. Just those two syllables were an effort.

He leaned back again, head pounding, eyes closed. For a while he seemed to be whirling dizzily about in space and he found he liked the sensation so he tried to prolong it. But it faded, and he opened his eyes again to stare bitterly at his paintings.

On an impulse he walked over and picked one up to examine it closely. It was wrong, all wrong. He should have done it better than this. It was chaotic, it was self-indulgent. He had claimed for it the virtue of self-expression, but it expressed nothing so much as inflated ideas and immaturity. He put his fist through it savagely. Then he took each one of his paintings, one by one, the best ones, the ones he had submitted to Boormans, and destroyed them carefully and methodically, one after another, with his bare hands at first and then with scissors.

Someone was tugging at his arm. She was yelling something at him, but he could not make out what, it was just a scream. She was trying to make him stop.

'Fuck off, bitch,' he said. But she still clung to him, trying to drag him away. He stared at her face, vaguely horrified. Her mouth was clearly forming definite words, but all he could hear was this high pitched roar. It was making the pain in his head crash furiously against his skull.

'Shut up!' he yelled. 'Shut up! Shut up! Shut up! Shut up!' He rammed her head against the wall each time he said it.

She screamed all the louder. He wanted to scream back at her. Her scream tore deep down inside him, letting loose all the frustrated rage he had kept insecurely bottled up there, setting it free. He felt as if he was being physically torn apart.

'Shut up!' he screamed back. If only he could make her SHUT UP!

He grabbed the scissors and stabbed her furiously in the face and throat. She screamed and thrashed and gurgled, and was quiet.

She fell heavily to the floor.

Swank slid down against the wall to sit beside her, his pounding head in his hands.

Then he lay down there and slept.

ALISON

From the window of the office Alison could see the castle, so-called, beneath the grey skies. Actually it was a mere tower, made higher by being set on a great mudpie of a mound, but none the less just an empty circle of stone. Beside it were the more modern buildings where the rest of the castle had once stood. They were Victorian institutional, dull and squat, with windows meant to let in light but not to be looked out of. They had once been a prison.

White-haired Mr Marlow came back into the room, and smiled constructively as he sat down.

'Shall we get on?' he said.

His office was a space with a desk in it, a chair on his side and two chairs on hers. On the wall was a clock that told the correct time. There was no other furniture. Mr Marlow pulled prematurely aged papers from a dusty folder. Alison kept quiet.

'You're our budding singer, aren't you?'

She nodded.

'So what have you been doing?'

'We've been practising a lot. Not that many gigs, though.'

'How many? In the past month.'

'. . . Three.'

'And what about the other thing?'

She pretended not to understand.

'You were going to bring me a list of the places where you had applied for work.'

'Oh. Well. I didn't actually make a list.' She saw his querying look. 'Actually,' she lied, 'I was cutting the ads out of the paper and I was going to give them to you, but after I'd been turned down for half a dozen it seemed pretty pointless going on so I threw them away.'

Mr Marlow had eyes that were as black as sockets in a skull. You never could tell for sure if he believed you. She had applied for no jobs whatsoever.

'Of course there is the problem of creative people fitting into the world of work,' he said, starting upon his regular routine. 'They do genuinely have difficulties that most people just do not understand. We have a young man in this very department . . .' Et cetera, et cetera. And so forth and so forth. Was he going to come crashing down on her with some edict that would force her into a job or else deprive her of her dole money, or was she going to be let off for another few months?

She said, 'We've been practising a lot. We're getting to be very good.'

'But then,' he went on, incorporating her comment effortlessly into his speech, 'so many people are able, with no doubt some sacrifice of their time and of themselves, to work normally during the day and confine their practising or their singing or their painting to their free hours. Or there are actors, people who need to have their days free for auditions and so forth, and work at night serving on tables or washing dishes. Trollope, I believe, used to do his writing early in the morning or on the train or during his lunch break, and he was a very successful man.'

He stopped abruptly, at the end of his paragraph, and looked at her as if she was now expected to say something.

'I quite agree,' she said. 'I *have* been looking. It's just, I don't really seem to have what they want.'

He nodded his head sympathetically.

'What, after all, if this were the nineteenth century, and there was no social security, and you had to either find a job or starve?'

Last time she had injudiciously confused him by suggesting she could have gone to the workhouse or else found herself a husband who was in work. This time she kept quiet until a tilt of his head and a raising of his eyebrows indicated he felt he had made his point.

'I see your point,' she said.

She calculated that at an hour per interview, say six interviews a day, thirty a week, over the course of a year he must make that speech approximately one thousand five hundred times.

She was developing an awesome headache which she knew would not disappear till she was safely away.

Because he was not just ruminating on like the grandfatherly old man he appeared to be. Those hollowed eyes, tired and watering slightly, were watching every shade of expression on her face.

'So,' he went on, 'we have to ask ourselves, just where and how do we come to terms with what we are forced by circumstance to recognise as the real world, the world of daily living?' He stopped and waited for her to make some suggestions.

'My band's doing quite well,' she said. 'I'm sure it's only a matter of time before we start earning some decent money.'

'How much money?' he demanded. 'Three hundred, four hundred pounds a week? Divided among the five of you? Minus expenses? Minus payments on your equipment? Or less than that?'

'Probably a little less at first.'

'Do the others have day jobs?'

'Some of them do.' Cautiously.

'So they will forego their share of the band earnings to give you a big enough wage to get you off the dole?'

Obviously not. It would be a five-way split of very little.

'No, I really see nothing for it but this.' He tapped the local paper which lay folded on his desk. 'Have you been looking at this?'

'Sometimes.'

He cupped his hands and leaned on them thoughtfully.

'I've been taking singing lessons you see,' she said.

He glanced at her, but otherwise made no response.

'And there's a lot of running around to do, trying to get gigs and things. We don't have any sort of manager, and I've sort of taken on that role myself. With it being my band.'

He toyed with his pencil.

'So it's not as if I'm sitting around all day doing nothing. I have applied for jobs but it seems a little pointless when you just keep getting turned down.'

He nodded his head.

She waited.

He seemed to consider.

She glanced at the clock.

He stood up abruptly and offered her his hand. 'Let's just see what happens then, shall we? You show me that we have made some serious effort at finding a job and we'll discuss it all properly next time.' He ushered her to the door and she was outside almost before she had even realised it was over.

Her legs and arms felt weak. She hurried away as fast as she could in case he called her back.

Even so, it was better to keep the old man happy and at least pretend she wanted to work. If he got together with some government department and fixed up an interview for her it would most certainly be for some job she could not refuse without getting her benefit cut.

So, without even pausing for lunch, to get it done with as quickly as possible, she went off to the Job Centre.

She had come here more than a dozen times when she had first left her previous job and had been partially serious about finding a new one. But it had not taken long to conclude that a Job Centre was a dreary, arid, defeated place, where you might certainly get bored, but only if you were very lucky or very normal would you get a job.

When Mr Marlow asked her why she did not go to the Job Centre more often and she replied that there did not seem to be much point, it was one of the few times when he did not treat her answers sceptically.

She found a card in the office workers' section. These rows of cards with their unexciting type and their dull, impersonal language were the worst things about the place. Looked at naïvely, each one was an offer of hope. More cynically, more realistically, each one offered a task filled with daily tedium or, more likely, a rebuff. She swore she would never willingly accept one of those jobs.

She took a number from the desk, and after some twenty minutes was called up to present her card.

The girl at the desk, not much older than Alison, phoned the company.

'Do you have good typing?' she asked Alison, looking up.

'Not really. I can get along all right. But it's two-finger stuff, really.'

It always took her five minutes to find each letter. She'd got into a habit of exaggerating the facts in trying to sell her band.

The girl hung up. 'They want someone who can type,' she said. 'I am sorry.'

Alison shrugged a half-smile, and hoped her eyes did not too clearly beacon her relief. She had caught the name of the company, and wrote it down on a scrap of paper as soon as she was in the street so she could present it to Mr Marlow, and that was that. Now her time was her own. She could think about lunch, and if she was sensible she would save some money by taking the bus home and eating there. She caught the bus.

The previous week she had paid a long-delayed visit to her aunt in Harrogate. Aunt Monica was an active, dogged woman married to a brusque, sharp-eyed man. The attachment of the aunt to the niece had recently seemed to vary in accordance with the claims that the niece could make for finding her place in the world. When Alison went from school to work with a minimum of trouble her aunt nodded with approval. When Alison began singing in a local club her aunt was clearly impressed, and a visit meant her dragging out stories of old singing stars who had made it big despite their early struggles. When Alison put her band together and abandoned night club melody for the commercial end of blues rock, her aunt took this as a mark of her determination and was prepared to admit her niece to her deepest confidences. And even after Alison left her job and started to live off the State, off the backs of hard-working people like her aunt and uncle, her aunt accepted it as a necessary, temporary, aberration. But as month after month went by, and neither a new job nor a number one hit record materialised, Aunt Monica seemed to become increasingly distant.

Not that anything specific was said. She just felt less obviously welcome in their house. All Alison could offer in her defence were the same hopes she had had six months before, with possibly a few extra disappointments. Aunt Monica was verging on polite and sympathetic contempt. For her, as with the DHSS, if you could not make money from your day-dreams you put them to one side and got down to earning a living.

There had been an affection between them since childhood, and if Aunt Monica was willing to allow principle to override that, then Alison was not going to readily forgive her disdain. She thought she would stop seeing her aunt for a while.

She got off the bus feeling depressed, and walked the street and a half home. With the instincts of her upbringing she had chosen the cheapest bedsit available in the most expensive area she could afford, hoping to graduate upwards. So while she lived in pleasant enough surroundings, leafy, well kept, on the edge of the city, her actual home was the tiny front room of a sixty-year-old cottage down a back street.

She had just about been able to stand it for the first couple of years. Now it was starting to gnaw at her.

Coming into the house she met the O'Leary going out. The O'Leary had the alarming habit of walking to the toilet or picking up the post completely unclothed, trusting that her great bulk and the house being full of women would free her from any charges of indecency. Alison knew nothing more off-putting early in the day than a naked O'Leary scratching herself on the landing.

The house would have held a small family with cosy comfort. Five strangers in such a space grated against each other endlessly. There had only been four when Alison moved in, but when a long-term tenant moved out of the big room upstairs, the landlord had divided the one big room into two tiny ones, charging the same big room rent for each. Landlords, after all, have to make a living like the rest of us.

Being in the front room, by the front door, Alison heard all their comings and goings. She had not been home long when she heard the great crash that announced the return of the Gibbs, and then her hacking smoker's cough as she dragged herself up the stairs. At about 5.15 p.m. the Miss Bottom would return from work and let herself in with the most furtive silence, and shortly after that the Hodge would also come home from work and slouch her way into the room at the back. The Miss Bottom was fortyish and had clearly given up on just about everything. The Hodge was young, thin, plain, and had as friends a set of women equally thin and plain who regularly stayed overnight.

They all hated each other with silent distaste.

Alison had worked out that if she got a job and saved all she could, she would easily have the downpayment for a flat within eighteen months, and have the rest paid off in five or six years. She could work for five or six years and sing in the evenings, just like they said she could. Easily. Then, after five or six years, when it was clear she was not going to get anywhere with this singing business, she would at least have a decent place to live in. That was sensible. That was what sensible people did. That was what sensible people knew to be best.

The O'Leary came back from wherever it was she had gone and stood panting on the doormat.

The O'Leary had probably once been sensible. Aunt Monica was incomparably sensible. And surely there was no one in the world more truly and totally sensible than the worn-down Miss Bottom.

In the evening she switched out the lights and listened to music over the headphones, a perfect cocoon of dark and sound, her only full and solitary escape. She should have been listening to Janis Joplin or Aretha Franklin. She could never be Janis, but that was what they were supposedly aiming at.

Her record collection contained a lot of such material, some of it bought early on out of love or admiration, some of it bought much more recently and half out of a sense of duty. Then there was '77 punk, which she had bought when all her friends were buying it and which she had drifted away from as she had lost touch with most of her old companions. From punk she wanted neither those harsh-edged rhythms nor the raucous brick-in-the-face force, but she did envy that power, that sense of being just across the boundary into loss of control.

So there was no escape in blues or punk, escape was only in Petula and Dusty and Cilla, love songs when she was not in love, full of a glow that she could not allow herself because such things were no longer fashionable; they had become the tinsely glamour of the mock elegant in their over-priced, sordid night spots. But nothing threatened her insecurity on those albums, nothing probed at her self-doubt and illuminated her feelings. Gentling release.

The next day there was 'running about' to do, hustling for the band, mostly without result. Then there was the gig.

It was their first gig in three weeks. There was a little bar which took bands from all over the north. They saved money by having you play two sets, but if they liked you they gave you steady work and they had a core of regulars who would talk about you to their friends. The place had not been designed as a bar, it had been converted from a restaurant. There was no dressing-room, only an office where they could throw their coats and things. And there was no proper soundcheck because no one ever seemed to show up there to let anyone in until just before it opened, so they finished setting up with the first customers staring at them, got individual bits and pieces checked out, and trusted to the guy at the board to get the mix right after the first song or two. But it was so good to be doing another gig.

They sat at a table at the front while the place partially filled up. They had a good hour to wait till their first set. Birch, the drummer, showed up with his new girlfriend, a small girl with short, dark hair. She sat trying to tease a comb through the tangle of his hair, which he always washed, dried, then left untouched, his natural curls tightening into a steadily expanding impenetrable frizz. Birch had been very moody lately, mostly over women, but at the party at the weekend he and this girl had been getting smashed together, trying to drink cider from the same bottle at the same time, and disappearing discreetly long before the night was over. So at least it seemed as if his problems there were over for a while.

Bassist Tony arrived alone and looking tired. Tony always looked tired. He was tall and narrow, and said little. When he did have a girl with him she was always extremely soft and beautiful. They liked to mother him because of his lost and helpless ways. Birch always looked just as sloppy as Tony did, but no one ever tried to mother Birch because he clearly knew he was sloppy, liked being sloppy, and meant to stay sloppy. Tony just looked as if he'd had trouble getting dressed in the morning. Like Alison, Tony was on the dole, but he went to job interviews quite regularly because they gave him something to do. He looked and acted so vague there was never any danger of anyone employing him.

The other two, Jonathan on keyboards and Peter on guitar, were completely different. For one thing, they were both strikingly normal, Peter looking as if he'd just been out shopping, and Jonathan as if he'd just got back from the office. Birch and Tony constantly put them down, each in his different way. Birch sneered openly at Jonathan's suits, and Tony did his silent smile when Peter said something particularly middle class. They were both up on the stage, earnestly fiddling about with the equipment. Every so often Tony had to come on chummy with Jonathan because he wanted him to fix up his decrepit amp.

Nerves, and even some shyness, locked them in a private circle of their own, but Alison kept an eye on the faces to see if there was anyone there she recognised from earlier gigs, any sign they were building up a following. There wasn't, of course. There was one particularly sharp-looking young man who stood alone at the bar all night and watched her singing with serious scrutiny. Maybe, she hoped, a journalist and publicity. Maybe, she also hoped, someone who would successfully pick her up and who would turn out to have all the right ideas and contacts that would make her into someone important. If he was a journalist he did not write anything that she had ever heard about, and although he stayed until their last song he disappeared immediately afterwards.

She enjoyed her singing. However anyone might criticise, no one could say that she did not have a good voice. The crowd began to cheer amiably enough, particularly as they got into the second set. They were a good, beery, enthusiastic bunch, mostly regulars. They were the ones who hated disco with a passion but had been equally bewildered by what punk rock had thrown at them in the last three or so years. They were true to their old tastes and their old favourites, and eager to reward any good band that was willing to provide them.

And her band were sounding good. She had put them on tape recently and had been disturbed by how ramshackle they had been. But that was on tape, without proper production or anything. It did not mean they sounded ramshackle live, and she could hear quite clearly that they did not. Birch and Tony were getting particularly tight, and a good rhythm section was worth more than any amount of slickness.

But Peter was clearly no blues guitarist. He was the kind of person who learnt the notes from the record and thought that was all there was to it. If you mentioned it to him he looked pained, and got ever more precise. She had no idea what she was going to do with Peter. He was far too nice a person to simply chuck out.

As the crowd warmed to her, she warmed to them. They encouraged her and she loosened up, let go of her grip on the mike stand, and began to put her heart into it. She and her audience, getting off on each other, like old friends getting a little drunk and a little rowdy together, sharing a few laughs, a little backchat, getting sentimental over old melodies.

She just hoped the management was watching so that she would be asked back.

Afterwards she strode about the empty bar, chatting with the staff, bright-eyed and full of herself. It was a charge that would last her into next week. She could go home in the dark, walk the quiet streets of her leafy suburb, and tell herself, 'Alison, you're doing all right.'

HIGH CULTURE

Swank ran across Ken and Julie outside Marks & Spencer and they decided they would go with him to Konnectic as it was probably going to rain. Swank looked pissed off, but there was no point in asking him why. Instead they started telling him about how Ken had gone home the night before with a tree.

'What do you mean, a tree?'

'I had a tree. I left it just outside the door. There was mud all over the place.'

'When I went over this morning he says to me, "Where's this tree come from?" And I said, "You brought it home with you last night." '

'I don't even remember!'

Swank admitted a grin.

'So he probably got it out of somebody's garden. It's just a little tree, like a big bush.'

'I must have been walking around with this tree . . .!'

'You had it over your shoulder. I said, "What's that for?" and you said, "It's a tree . . ." '

At Konnectic, Nick was sitting in a battered leather armchair watching a video. Swank sat down to watch it with him, but Ken and Julie had not been to Konnectic for a while and were intrigued by the exhibition. It was a big room, sparse walls painted a grubby white and the floor just bare wood. Someone had taken doll's clothing, baby's clothing, anything small and wearable, put them on wire frames to make them stand up, and scattered them about the floor. Ken and Julie wandered around hand in hand, in hushed fascination. It was like an array of toy soldiers come to life. Or like when you open the door and switch on the light too fast for everything to make it back to the cupboard.

Lesley came in from the back-room with a new pot of tea.

'Oh shit,' she said, seeing them, and sent them round the back to wash themselves a couple of cups.

'Make it three!' she called, seeing Swank sitting there as well.

On the video a naked man was standing in thoughtful repose while two other naked men poured paint over him. The soundtrack was demented Kraftwerk, a wind-up synthesiser with all its insides erupting, and every so often a harsh Germanic voice would break through reading a weather forecast beneath a hail of interference. There was an abrupt halt, and a girl in a white dress, all out of focus, stumbled along the bank of a river beneath blurred leafy trees. Then the noise started again, only now the first man had wrapped a towel around his head and was helping the second man cover the third man in peanut butter.

'Fucking weird,' said Swank.

'I could do that,' sneered Ken, arriving with the sugar. 'Anyone could do that. Load of rubbish.'

'Of course anyone could do it,' said Lesley. 'That's the whole point.'

'Take your picture?' said Julie, getting out her new camera.

'Come on, Nick, we're going to get our picture taken.'

Nick abandoned the video, and the two of them climbed on the desk and clung to each other while Julie took their photo.

'How was New York anyway?' asked Swank, turning down the sound and coming for some tea.

'Terrible,' said Lesley. 'I didn't get laid. I wanted to get laid by some blond American.'

'We had this room in the Chelsea Hotel,' said Nick. 'And we thought it was the one where Sid had stabbed Nancy, and Lesley was lying on the floor where they were supposed to have found her and I was pretending to be Sid. It was great.'

They could just see Lesley groaning under the sink with a big grin on her face.

Nick went on, 'Then we found out it wasn't Sid's room at all.'

After a while Ken and Julie said they had to leave, but Swank hung around for a while, reading the art magazines they had brought back from New York.

'Ken's right,' he said eventually. 'Anyone can do this. Just most people can't be bothered.'

'It's more a psycho-social perceptual set,' said Nick. 'It seldom even reaches the question of actual motivation.'

'Yeh,' agreed Swank.

'Why don't you do something?' said Lesley. 'Not painting or anything. Just something interesting.'

'Why don't we put him on tomorrow night?' suggested Nick. 'We still need a second event.' The gallery had regular nights of Performance Art.

'All right,' said Lesley. 'Tomorrow night, 7.30. Don't tell us in advance, we want to be surprised as well.'

She calmly entered it in her book and Nick took his coffee and went to rewind the video.

'Yeh, all right,' said Swank. 'Tomorrow night.'

Later that afternoon Swank took the bus out to the University, very much new ground for him.

Swank had been picked up in a pub by Nick and Lesley because he 'looked right', the pair taking People As Art to its logical conclusion and acquiring the latest works for occasional exhibition: drinking tea or watching videos. Swank was attracted by their way of doing bizarre things in a wholly matter of fact manner. Their gallery, so austere to the public view, had a behind-the-scenes back room filled with a wondrous assortment of junk. Broken furniture, clothes, a kitchen sink. Fifty copies of one Ricki Lee Jones album resulting from a brain-fogged, night-time raid on a record shop. Over two hundred paperback books without covers that happened to have come their way. A porcelain box marked 'Pills' contained pills, and another one hidden in a dressing-table drawer contained other things. Swank had affected to sneer, but more and more it became a place to drop in at.

Swank had been there one afternoon when a group of students had come in and it turned out they were all from the same theatre class.

'What, putting on plays and things, or just reading about them?' Swank had wanted to know.

They were not too sure, it being near the beginning of term, but they talked it over and concluded that they thought a play was going to be performed at some point.

Swank had written a play. It was called *Mediatrix*, and he had sat down one night and written the whole thing without stopping. It had felt like it was being written for him or through him. Reading it over he was certain it was better than anything he had ever done.

'You should come and talk to Peter,' they said, their earnest faces glowing with open wonder. You just never knew what you were going to find in this Konnectic place.

So Swank went to talk to Peter.

It was a newish University, mostly built in the sixties, all odd shapes and mismatched levels, as if the architects had suffered brain damage at an early age and were unable to make visual sense of their environment. Swank found it attractively grotesque.

He followed the signs with a fair degree of success, and eventually met some people from the theatre class carrying each other along the corridors. One would be hoisted above their shoulders, flat out as if for a funeral, and carried in solemn procession a few hundred yards, then let down and another lifted up. They all had stolid, mock-serious expressions, but the girls kept giving it away by giggling.

'Here's Swank,' they said, seeing Swank. They forgot all about what they were doing and crowded around him. 'This is Peter.' 'This is Swank.'

'Yes. Marvellous,' said Peter, holding out his hand.

'Hello,' mumbled Swank.

They took him back to the Workshop, a large concrete bunker well away from the seminar rooms. There was a low, makeshift stage at one end and an interesting array of ladders, lights, and boards at the other. Another dozen or so students were putting on shoes and sweaters, the class apparently just ending. Swank nodded hello to a girl he recognised, Mary-Jane, and leant against the wall to wait.

'So . . .' declared Peter as the room cleared. Energy washed about him in waves. He seemed to have concentrated his entire essence in a dramatic, rock-hard exoskeleton. 'Shall we go upstairs for coffee?'

They went up to the lounge, eight of them in total, the

go-getters of the theatre class with Mary-Jane tagging along. Peter paid for Swank's coffee. 'This is the play,' Swank said, as they sat down.

Peter rested his feet on the table and sipped his drink. '*Mediatrix*,' he declaimed. 'It's about the media?'

'No, it's about . . . a girl. That's just the name.' He was not at all sure what Mediatrix meant. It had just appeared in his head along with the rest of the play.

Peter leafed through it. No one seemed to know what to say. Eventually two of them started talking together and the rest joined in, relieved. They kept glancing at Swank to show him they did not want him to feel excluded. Swank drank his coffee, then went back to the canteen and stole a bun.

As he sat down again Peter rolled up the play decisively.

'You know, I think it would be marvellous if we could get you to act in one of our plays. Can't you see him in Brecht?'

They all stared at him enthusiastically. Swank scowled back.

Afterwards Mary-Jane suggested he come along with her to the student newspaper, the *Leveller*. He knew Mary-Jane from a party. She was somehow, strangely and indefinably, old fashioned. She was not his type, but there was a touching earnestness about her. She had been wasting her mind and body on some beatnik, an anarchist-socialist whose great complaint was State Control and whose great panacea was State Ownership. He wondered if she was still seeing him.

'So . . . you know Gerry and them?' she began.

'No, not really. We just met at Konnectic.'

'. . . Oh.'

The student newspaper office was a large room littered with desks and paper. Someone was typing obsessively, the phone rang unanswered, and four different conversations were going on at once. She took him over to two young men who seemed to be having an argument.

'I don't need a drug, I need a final solution,' one was saying. 'Archetypal resonances!'

'I don't get around, I don't fall in love much,' retorted the other. 'Alienation!'

'Alienation?!' cried the first, flinging up his arms. 'Alienation is a cliché. Alienation is the devalued shilling of last decade's untenured sociologist!'

'This is Swank,' Mary-Jane broke in.

'Oh, hello,' they said, stopping short and looking at each other as if they had forgotten what they were talking about.

'Coloured condoms!' gurgled a voice from the corner, and a little fat person doubled up with laughter.

'That's Greg,' said Mary-Jane. Then, indicating the disputants, 'This is Doug, this is Paul.'

'So . . .' said Doug, archetypal resonances, looking Swank up and down. 'How do you feel about the crisis of capitalism?'

'Rubbish!' shouted Paul, before Swank could think of a response. 'Rubbish! What about the Diocletian revolution? What about the sixteenth-seventeenth-century inflation spiral and the decline of the gentry?'

'What decline? What gentry?' demanded Doug.

'Love comes in spurts!' chortled Greg over in the corner.

Swank took advantage of the unwatched phones to call around to see if anyone had any idea what had become of Lita, who had not been home in two nights. He did not really want to care whether anyone had seen her or not. It infuriated him that she thought she could make him suffer.

Someone he phoned said they had seen her at a party last night, but she had gone off before they had a chance to speak. No one else knew anything at all. Swank hung up, hating himself for his weakness.

'Swank, old man,' said Doug, appearing at his side, 'shall we retire to the pub?'

They retired to the pub, along with Mary-Jane and Greg. It was just on the next floor. The stairs were made of concrete, and they were covered in water because the flat roof above them had been stylishly edged so that the building would look more angular and when it rained hard the water had nowhere else to go.

Greg was reciting his *Monty Python*. He had started with the complaint contra tourists as they left the office, and by the time they reached the pub was well into the opening scenes of Hell's Grannies. The pub, although designed to be fiercely impersonal, had succumbed ruefully to a decade and a half of beery humanity and was warm and noisy. They sat down and ordered.

'It's all Fellini's *Satyricon*,' said Greg, interrupting himself unexpectedly and looking about. 'It's just a larger perspective.'

'What?' asked Swank.

'He's in Film Studies,' said Doug. 'Ignore him.'

'The illusion of incoherence that embellishes the underlying continuity,' said Greg. 'In life, I mean. It's Fellini's genius that he makes explicit that continuity by relentlessly piling on the incoherence.'

'Tell me,' said Doug, sipping his Campari, 'do you feel the Church has a legitimate role to play in the political arena, or do you think they should just sit on their arses contemplating the clouds?'

'I dunno,' said Swank. 'I never go to church.'

'It's a cancer,' asserted Paul. 'A political cancer that devours spirituality and makes gross the sublime. Allow politics into the Church and the whole structure will decay from the inside.'

'Not true, Paul, not true,' insisted Doug. 'What's important are The People, all those insignificant little people to whom the Church is just a smug snug cliquey club. Their whole lives are the victims of politics. The Church has to show itself capable of countering that victimisation.'

'That's what I said. Let politics in and it takes over and makes everything else submit to it. So eventually only Marxist materialists can get to heaven and candlesticks are beaten into weapons for the class war.'

'Class war, yes. Class war. Not a Church of secluded comfort for the middle classes with their big houses and their big cars. Class war. The gospel for the poor.'

'Pure bigotry. Does a man's car exclude him from salvation? Or the fact that he is able to house and feed his children? Does it?'

'It's not a question of exclusion, Paul, it's a question of education. Are we going to let them sleep cocooned in their blissful never-never land or are we going to use the Church to confront them with the realities of the real world? *There* is the point, Paul, right there!'

'Are we going to swamp the unifying truth of the divine in the divisive rhetoric of politicised humanity? *That's* the point, right there!'

'Well ask him, ask Swank. He's not your middle class churchgoer. Ask him what he thinks.'

They both looked at Swank.

'I dunno,' he said. 'I never really thought about it.'

There was a contemplative pause.

'A dinosaur,' recited Greg into the silence, 'is narrow at one end, fat in the middle, and narrow again at the other end.'

They turned on him with two crushing stares.

'Yes Greg,' said Doug. 'But what about the pterodactyl?'

Paul nodded seriously, but then began to look vaguely worried.

'Of course, a pterodactyl is not strictly a dinosaur,' he said.

Darkness was advancing, and the question arose of what they were going to do with the evening. Swank assumed that, being students, they would all have homework to do, but he was evidently wrong for the discussion was, Shall we go see a film? or Shall we go to a party and get drunk? Mary-Jane was inclined to the merits of drunkenness and Swank was inclined to agree, seeing that Lita was making herself unavailable. But the others wanted to go to a film, and that was finally what they did.

They went in Doug's car, a shiny red Porsche with new licence plates, a gift from his parents. There was still the question of which film to go to. Greg favoured *Ilsa, She-Wolf of the SS* at the Venus. There were cries of sexist, but Greg was adamant.

Finally Doug said, 'All right, yes, it's sexist. But sexism is a fact of life. You have to face up to that. And life must be understood in all its many facets.'

So it was agreed.

While Greg was leaning forward exchanging blows with the front seats, Swank was beginning a cautious interrogation of Mary-Jane to see if she was still seeing that other bloke and if she could be fairly easily detached. The answers seemed to be yes and probably. He did not think, for reasons that he could never have found words for, that she slept with her boyfriend very often. That made his work easier in some ways, harder in others.

He felt bored with her already. He noticed that the conversation had died down in the front.

'I'll tell you something,' he said to Doug and Paul, 'about what you were saying before in the pub.'

'Church and politics, you mean?' asked Doug.

'I think they've got a fucking nerve. There they are with their

Oxford educations and their degrees in religion, what gives them the right to think I need them to feel sorry for me? What gives them the right to lump me in as one of the poor and humble masses? I'm not part of anyone's fucking masses, and being on the dole doesn't make me poor and miserable. And it's all for no other reason than to lure people into church to protect the priests' own jobs. They've got a fucking nerve, whatever their politics.'

'See,' said Paul, looking pleased. 'Alienation.'

The film was about this beautiful butch female Nazi who had been sent to a concentration camp to supervise the experiments, all frigid self-repression with huge tits just about bursting out of her tightly buttoned uniform. (Chortles from Greg, rude comments from the others.) Then there were these prisoners that she slept with – every night she took a different one to her bed and every morning she had him shot because she was unsatisfied with his performance. (Chuckle, jeer, giggle.) But there was one man, an American, the one leading the escape attempt, whom she had back night after night. How did he do it? the other prisoners wanted to know. What was his secret? 'Well, I'll tell you,' drawled the American. ('Ssh, ssh,' urged Paul, and the whole cinema went silent.) 'I have trained myself to maintain an erection for hours at a time without ejaculating.'

'Oh God,' complained Mary-Jane.

'Haw Haw Haw!' Greg was going, 'Haw Haw Haw!'

And then they were booted out for making so much noise.

They walked down the street with Greg still chuckling over the film. Paul was arguing that anal complexes were more important than Oedipal complexes because their effects were self-reinforcing throughout a person's life, while Doug was arguing that white mice knew nothing of complexes of any sort and mankind's real problem was their refusal to elevate greed to its rightful status. There was still the matter of what to do with the rest of the night. Another pub seemed the best idea. Doug said he knew one that was all bring your own sawdust and be careful who you look at, so they went there.

As they gave him a lift home Swank sounded out Mary-Jane again on her coming in with him. But he had been making only reasonable progress with her all night, and ultimately she refused. They let him out at the top of his street, they called goodbye, and Doug drove doggedly away at great speed.

'Fucking nutters,' muttered Swank as he staggered down the road.

Home these days was a third floor flat in an aged, smallish building, two narrow rooms filled with mouldy clothes and unwashed dishes. The late post, he saw, had brought a letter from the TV rental company, forwarded from his last place. He wondered who there could possibly know his new address. He had sold the TV weeks ago.

There was no sign that Lita had been home.

Arguing was going on in the flat upstairs, Tom and Marcie's place. Tom was an artist specialising in abstract miniatures which he sold commercially for impressive prices. Tom called them pure shit and sniggered behind the backs of the people who bought them. He used all the money from them to finance his video experiments, which were not such a success.

Swank did a cup of instant soup and tore up some bread to put in it. He fiddled with the radio, wanting something to distract him, but there was only Radio Two or people babbling away in Danish.

By the time he had finished his soup the row upstairs had stopped and he thought he could probably manage to sleep.

There was a knock at the door.

'Switch off the light,' hissed Marcie as she pushed past him. 'If he thinks you're in he'll know I'm here.'

Swank shrugged, closed the door, and switched off the light.

'Do you want to sleep here tonight?' he asked. ''Cos I couldn't find Lita, and Mary-Jane wouldn't.'

'Hush,' pleaded Marcie, and Swank threw himself down on the couch to wait for the inevitable pounding on the door.

The pounding came, along with much shouting and kicking. Someone else opened a door and gave Tom hell for making so much noise, and eventually he slunk back upstairs. They heard his door slam.

'What's going on, anyway?' asked Swank.

'He filmed us,' wept Marcie.

Thrashing bodies.

'Filmed you?'

'Filmed us fighting last night. He had his little video camera whirring away on the top shelf, and then he sits me down tonight when I'm trying to be nice and smooth things over and he says, "Watch this," and it's us fighting. And every so often he freezes it and points out how idiotic my remarks are or how stupid I look or how fat I'm getting. I'm going to kill him. I'll use a knife and a pillow while he's asleep.'

Swank was intrigued.

'Is he going to sell it?' he asked.

'Sell it?! If he does! If he dares!!'

'He probably wouldn't,' said Swank, just to calm her down. But the idea fascinated him. Maybe he could use it in a play.

'Do you want to go to bed or don't you?' he asked.

Marcie sniffed. 'Can I have something to eat first?'

'I've got some soup.'

'Yeh, okay. Give me some bread to dunk in it. I don't know what they put in soup these days. It's certainly not chickens.'

Swank did not wake up till about noon. Marcie had already left and Lita had not yet shown up. That was too bad. He had hoped Lita would turn up while Marcie was still in bed so he would have the pleasure of seeing them fight. He thought Lita was rather overdoing the running about, but at least if she took up with someone else it would save him the trouble of ditching her.

He had arranged to go back out to the University to see Peter in the afternoon. He ate a quick breakfast, shaved, put on the cleanest shirt he could find, and set off for the bus stop.

Swank had told Peter that he needed some advice on how to fix up the play now it was written; practical things, technicalities of staging that needed to be incorporated into the script, spots where the pacing was off or something. He didn't know. He'd have to see.

Peter was waiting for him in his office. He sat Swank down and thumped a pile of booklets down in front of him.

'These are some other plays I'm looking at,' he announced, conversationally.

Swank looked around at the makeshift office, noticing the table instead of a desk, the chairs that were not the right height.

Clearly theatre did not get top priority around here. Maybe that was a good thing. It should make them less obnoxious.

'That top one's about Kennedy,' said Peter. 'It's about how people can remember where they were and what they were doing on the day Kennedy died.'

He paused dramatically. Swank realised he was supposed to ask what Peter had been doing on the day Kennedy died.

'Yeh?' he replied, thinking he should have said, 'Who?'

'Well now,' started Peter, all business, sitting down and taking out Swank's manuscript. He thumbed through it crossly. 'I would like to go through this with you, as you suggested. There are the makings of an interesting play here.'

Swank rubbed his nose, sniffing.

'In places you're just a touch heavy-handed. A little rhetorical. Reality's not like that, is it?' His attention wandered over Swank's clothes. 'Most people's reality. I'm not saying your own reality is all it could or should be. You must express your own reality. That's what a play is all about, the reality of the individual dramatically and powerfully expressed. I'm just thinking that for most people it could seem a touch heavy-handed.'

'I was thinking of more technical things,' said Swank, after some minutes of this.

'Of course . . . Well then, this here that you've called Act Two. It really doesn't fit in with the rest of the play.'

'Yes it does.'

'No, you see, it doesn't. It destroys the cohesion, the necessary flow. Drama must flow, it flows from the opening word, from the opening gesture, and it never stops flowing until the final curtain descends. The events of the play must be like a ship carried irresistibly forward by that surging momentum.' He picked up his pen to illustrate a ship carried irresistibly forward by the surging momentum. 'Look at your main characters. It's them we want to know about. Not all this other stuff.'

'But they're in Act Two all the way through. They're in Act Two more than in the other acts.'

'Yes. They are. That's right.' He seemed genuinely surprised. 'But even so . . .'

Swank did not know what to make of this. He had come here expecting useful ideas, not this academic word-wanking.

'Or,' Peter went on, ignoring Swank's cold stare, 'let us keep Act Two, but let us emphasise the disruption of the flow, emphasise the incoherence. Take the middle section out of Act Three, for example, and exchange it with the opening of Act One.'

This was a waste. Just getting out of bed to come here was a waste. He would have simply snatched the play back except that he still had hopes, reasonable or not, of them performing it.

Peter's flow had ceased and he had his hands clasped in front of him staring with furrowed brow at the wall.

'Well I'll certainly get back to you as soon as I can,' he said standing up, making an effort to show he had not been irritated. Swank allowed himself to be led to the door. 'Sorry I dragged you all the way out here. How's the weather? Rain holding off, I hope?'

'Yeh,' said Swank.

'Well, cheerio.'

'See ya.'

That was a waste.

The corridor was suddenly full of students, although no bells had sounded. Swank could feel them staring at him as they crowded past, but they refused to meet his eye. He caught a glimpse of Doug and Mary-Jane in the distance and hurried up a nearby flight of stairs so as to avoid them. He found his way outside and stood a moment, relieved at the coolness.

That was a fucking waste.

Angry and scornful, he ignored the buses and walked back into town, walking on eggs made of human skulls and smashing every one.

Once in the city centre he phoned Julie from a phone box and discovered that Lita was there.

'You've been phoning all over the place for me, Swank. I've got a life of my own to lead, you know. Just who the fuck do you think you are?'

'You sow. You fucking cunt.'

They hung up on each other.

Swank took his knife and prised off the top of the dialling mechanism, then tore loose everything inside. He surveyed his efforts. It did not look like much. He scratched at the paintwork for a bit, considering, but finally contented himself with a good kick and left.

He had not forgotten that he had agreed to appear at Konnectic tonight. And did he have a con for them. They were going to be so pissed off with him. His face relaxed for the first time that day, and he set off to a friend's house to borrow some rope.

Swank had never been to one of these Konnectic events, and was surprised at the size of the crowd. All the little clothes figures had been cleared away, the events being scheduled inbetween the regular exhibitions, and in their place were a mattress with white sheets, some packets of food, and a make-shift shower with a clear plastic curtain around it. Several people greeted him, Nick and Lesley, Doug and Paul; over the heads he could see Mary-Jane. He stopped to chat a little. But there were none of his regular friends here so he just wandered about waiting for something to happen.

Eventually it was time to begin. The crowd gathered around the mattress and a man and a woman got beneath the sheets.

An alarm clock rang. The man switched it off. They got up, took off their night clothes (they were wearing tidy white underwear), the man put on a suit and the woman put on a dress, and then they ate some Corn Flakes. The man kissed the woman goodbye and went off to work. The woman made the bed. Then she took off dress and underwear, got into transparent plastic top and leggings so she would not get wet, and went to take a shower. She soaped the plastic luxuriously while a grey pool of water spread itself out across the floor. She came out of the shower, removed the plastic clothes, put on her normal clothes, and swept those parts of the floor not yet wet. Then the man came back. They had tinned meat for dinner, got back into their nightclothes, got back on to the mattress, and wrapped themselves in the sodden sheets. End of show.

Everyone applauded.

Helpers began to clear up, and Lesley gave Swank a wave to tell him he was on next.

Swank felt rather bewildered. It had been very nice watching some girl take her clothes off, but whatever it was that made the whole thing more than trivial pretence had completely gone by him. He heard someone say she thought it was rather clichéd, too much like something or other done somewhere or other by someone else. Maybe then, this was simply an off night. He could not imagine that people regularly came to see something like that. Well it would be even more off when he had finished.

Mary-Jane was edging her way towards him, pretending not to see him so she could bump into him by accident. But he was saved by Lesley who told him they were ready.

Two largish pipes ran across the room near the ceiling, painted yellow. Swank took the chair from behind the desk and put it beneath them. He took off his jacket and hung it over the back of the chair, took the thick rope from the carrier bag he had brought with him, stood on the chair and threw the rope over the nearest pipe. Then he grasped both ends of the rope and hung from it. Just hanging there, looking over their heads. His arms began to tire and he let himself down. He rested a moment, then did it again. Then again.

He wondered just how long he would be able to get away with it. It could not be very exciting watching some idiot swinging from a pipe. Soon they would start getting restless and begin to suspect they were being conned.

He did it again.

He hung from the pipe twelve times in succession and they were still seriously watching.

He gave up and stepped down off the chair. Everyone applauded.

He stuffed the rope back in the bag, defeated.

'It was rather like what that woman was doing in Brighton,' he heard someone say. 'Except that there there was a feminist element which gave it rather more texture. This had something of a macho feel to it which was a little offensive, but the purpose I think was deprecatory rather than a glorification.'

He put on his jacket.

'Oh. Hello,' said Mary-Jane, bumping into him.

'Hello,' he said, and left.

So who the fuck knew what was what in this world? He could have taken a bunch of housewives out of Tesco's to that show and they would all have said it was rubbish and they would all have been completely right. Yet they probably bought bland syrupy soul albums and read endless romance novels and spent all their days trying out floor polishes, so what the fuck did they know? Those people at Konnectic tonight, they thought they were *it*. They thought they were the artistic élite, the ones who knew precisely what was what. So what the fuck did he know? Dress up in the sharpest styles, know all the latest rules and look with scorn on those who don't, and read the *Guardian* to get that authentic proletarian ethos.

Well bollocks to them. He knew where he was at. He would go his own way, thank you, and bollocks to them each and every one. He reached his flat and slammed the door, locking them all out.

Some time passed before he began to notice that things were not quite normal. In fact, things were missing. Bits and pieces of things. Lita-type things. She must have been here.

He went over to look in the cupboard. All her clothes were gone.

Well that was no loss.

All of her records and books were gone. There were no more unwashed pairs of tights coiled up in unexpected places, no more female magazines on the floor by the bed. She had even taken her very own cup and her very own breakfast bowl.

Well that was no loss either.

Half-a-dozen of his records were gone, too, and some of his clothes.

All that was left of her were some empty shampoo bottles in the bathroom. He opened the window and threw them into the street. Then he found a pair of shoes she had missed. He threw those out of the window as well. He was beginning to feel pretty good again.

Maybe he could root up Rick and John and they could go and get drunk.

The theatre class did a play about Vietnam.

OUT OF REACH

Rick's band, Snuff Flix, had got a gig playing support for a local heavy metal band, Trojan Whores. The girlfriend of Trojan's bass player knew the daughter of the person in charge of renting out the small community hall. This girl had got them a good price on the place but had also talked Snuff Flix on to the bill because her sister was going out with the brother of Snuff Flix's drummer.

The hall was a dusty little hole behind a church, almost impossible to find. Snuff Flix arrived well in time to set up their equipment only to find Trojan Whores already on the stage doing a soundcheck. There were three of them, all with long hair and droopy moustaches like ancient Saxons in Victorian engravings, and they had a colourful backdrop of a stallion mounting a mare. They played each song through at least twice, stopping every minute or so to confer with the soundman and waiting while he made copious notes on levels and things and then asked them to play it again.

Snuff Flix and their half-dozen followers stood in a glum little group while several rather straight-looking people sat around giving them funny looks.

Come 7.30 when the doors were supposed to open, Trojan Whores were just about satisfied. Snuff Flix were given ten minutes to set up their gear in front of Trojan's, and then band and friends were kicked out into the lobby to wait with the proletariat.

'I suppose we'll have to pay to get in, too,' said Rick.

The girl in charge, whose father had lent her the money to

rent both hall and bands, pushed him through the door and slammed it in his face.

Swank turned up with Carrie, and Mark turned up with Kim, and George turned up alone. In a recent moment of humour, George, would-be famous promoter of this parish, had declared himself a mere groupie, but tonight he was getting ideas above his station and was talking of forming his own band with himself as singer – about as likely an ambition as Nigel Dempster working for *Sounds*.

Mark had been digging up old Yoko Ono albums and was telling everyone how wonderful they were. Mark's latest band had recently split up when the drummer's wife made him quit and the guitarist moved to Manchester. There had been talk about him somehow fitting into Swank's band, Out Of Reach, but now he was teaming up with four other guys, fourteen and fifteen year olds that no one else knew, and was rumoured to be calling them the Naked Girls.

The doors were finally opened and they tumbled back into the hall. Snuff Flix got in free but their friends were supposed to pay, which they did not, of course.

The band got on stage and began tuning their guitars. Although things were already running forty-five minutes late, there were still only fifteen paying customers. The guy at the sound desk had switched everything on then gone for a drink.

'This is a fucking shitty set up,' said Rick into the mike.

Trojan Whores' drums alone occupied half of the already tiny stage. Snuff Flix's drums took up most of the space in front of them, and Rick, never the least physical singer in town, had a strip of stage two foot by three to move about in.

The drummer rattled about on his kit a little, all four looked at each other to see if they were ready, then they started into the first song.

The sound was astonishing. Its very crudity inspired awe. You could hear the guitar, hugely distorted, blasting out louder than even the deafest HM fan could bear, and a feeble clatter of drums in the background. Rick could have been miming and the bass player might just as well have gone home to visit his mother. None of them could hear what they were supposed to be playing, they weren't even sure if the monitors had been switched on.

They stopped before the song was half through and Rick voiced some more of his disgust. The band's followers applauded, amused by the chaos, but everyone else had retreated to the back. Most of them were only there because they were friends or relatives of Trojan Whores, and even the bravest among them were already seeking saner havens.

They did two more songs, which sounded no better than the first. The party had moved to a private room by the lobby where the booze was kept; no one was paying any attention to these appalling weirdos on stage. They got through a fourth song, and then Rick kicked the mike away in disgust.

'Come on, Rick. Give us a show!' taunted his mates.

'Fuck this,' he retorted. He jumped down off the stage and told the band to pack up.

'Fucking shit-hole.' He stormed out to the partying and grabbed hold of the girl in charge.

'Oh. Have you finished?' she said.

He dragged her into the lobby and raged at her. She just stared back at him in shock. She was already getting drunk and was not at all prepared for anything like this.

'Jesus, I thought Sandy was looking after that,' she said. Sandy was the soundman.

There was a youth at the table to take the money, the only other person in the lobby, and Rick ordered her to send him off to find Sandy, which she quickly did. Then she fled back to her friends who were all wanting to know when Trojan Whores were going to play. Rick noticed the abandoned money for the first time, pocketed it, and took off back into the hall.

'Come on,' he spluttered. 'Let's get going.'

They'd already just about loaded up the van but there was some trouble starting at the door where Trojan followers were trading sneers with Snuff Flix followers. Then one of the girls with Trojan, falling about drunk, went sprawling against Derek who grabbed at her as much to stop her hitting the ground as anything, and her shirt was torn and a breast exposed. Rick was running around telling everyone to hurry up and get going and they thought he was just trying to avoid a fight but he kept saying no, he'd ripped off Trojan and they had to *move.* So everyone was pushed into the van and they finally got away with not so much as a split lip and forty-four quid in the black.

They all had a good laugh at that when Rick calmed down enough to explain what had happened. Although some of them would have preferred the money *and* the fight.

Out of Reach had Swank singing and playing a bit of guitar, Julie on bass, Julie's boyfriend, Ken, doing most of the real guitar work, and a kid called Ron playing the drums. Swank had wanted Carrie to be in the band as well but she had refused, saying she was not 'musical' enough.

Ron lived with his parents in the suburbs and his house had a large shed cum tiny garage at the bottom of the garden. It had no proper lighting but did have electricity and was always more or less empty and, as long as the band confined their noise to certain hours, his parents let them practise there. Ron's mother provided them with the occasional snack, but in private she expressed some disapproval at the sort of people Ron was getting himself mixed up with. Ron had also acquired a beaten-up Bedford van which had been adopted as official transport. So all in all young Ron was a very useful chap, despite being so fat.

Equally as useful, and much better looking, was Julie, whose lucky break in the job market had brought her completely new equipment, as well as a new amp for Ken when his suddenly expired. People wondered what she saw in Ken, who was only average looking while she was stunning. She had taught him how to dress, and even now she always looked far tougher than he did, like a dark-haired barbarian warrior queen with some risen from the ranks conscript.

Saturday after lunch was a regular practice session, and the day after the Trojan Whores fiasco Swank and Carrie turned up just as Ken was backing the van into the driveway.

'I thought I'd bring it over for our gig on Thursday night,' Ken said. 'We won't be needing it before then.

'We should stop lending it out to Rick and them,' he went on. 'He drives like a maniac. One of us should drive it at least, if we lend it out.' He went into the house to get something to drink.

The back garden was already reverberating to Julie's bass, playing some tune of her own while Ron bashed away at something entirely different. It was dark in the shed till their eyes adjusted. Julie had her back to them and did not know they had arrived till she caught Ron's nod of hello.

' 'Lo, Swank,' she said, turning. 'Like my new bass?'

Swank would probably not have noticed if she had not mentioned it, but once it was pointed out to him he was suitably appreciative. 'Where'd you get that?' he asked.

'Stole it,' she said, pleased with herself. 'Me and Mick.' Mick was the drummer from Snuff Flix. He had nordic features and liked to show off his muscles. 'You know that hotel ballroom where they have all those cabaret-type bands? We were going by there this morning and they were loading some band's gear into a van. They were all inside for a minute so we jumped into the van and grabbed this. Not bad, eh?'

'Pretty good,' grinned Swank. 'Looks brand new, too.'

'Yup. I'm going to paint it, though.'

'Yeh, disguise it a bit.'

She broke into a new torrent of notes, with Ron joining in. They stopped for a moment when the door opened, but she started up doodling again when she saw it was only Ken.

Carrie made herself comfortable while Swank messed about plugging the mike into Julie's old bass amp and Ken tuned up his guitar.

'Well?' said Julie, coming to a sudden halt. 'What shall we play?'

Ken crashed into the first few chords of some Iggy Pop, so they played that. Then they did some Pistols, not because they did any Pistols in their set but just because they were old favourites.

'We should do some originals,' said Swank, after Pretty Vacant, Bodies, Wanna Be Me, 16, and New York. So they did one of their own songs, but then Julie felt like doing some old Adverts songs because she had just been listening to the album, so they did Bombsite Boy and Safety in Numbers.

Swank was just thinking they had better get serious and run through a few of the songs in their set when three of Ron's friends arrived and Ron's mother came down with glasses of Coke.

'Where were you this morning, anyway?' Ken asked Julie as soon as he had her to one side.

Julie put her hands on him and started to get sensuous with her mouth. She did not answer his question.

Carrie was feeling dispirited. One of Ron's friends had got himself a car which was needing a bit of work, and Swank was deeply involved in the general discussion, for all his minimal knowledge about cars. Clearly there was no real practising going to be done that day. She went outside and sat on the grass.

The man who lived next door stared openly at her pink hair, so she gave him frequent glances of dislike till he went away.

After a while everyone started coming out of the shed. Ken and Julie were going off somewhere and Swank was going off with Ron to another of Ron's friends, so Carrie trailed along with him. At the house of Ron's friend they all said hello to mum on the way in, and Ron's friend led them up to his room. Mum stared after them dubiously.

In his room was a huge old gramophone of the kind that played only 78s and you had to change the needle after every couple of records. Ron's friend had a big collection of old 78s, and he put on Hound Dog which scratched away authentically – the simple wonder of such a museum piece actually working quite making up for there being no fresh supply of needles to replace the ones that had worn out in 1953. After the demonstration he closed up the treasured antique and played the 78s on his modern stereo, where they sounded marginally better.

'Look at this,' he said, taking drapes from his wardrobe. 'This is the real thing. You can't get them like this, not cheap. Got it off my dad.'

Carrie thought, fucking Teds, and wished she'd stopped home. But Swank seemed to be in a tolerant mood and it was soon clear that they would be here for the rest of the afternoon.

'Yeh, groovy,' she said, when Ron's friend showed her his prized Billy Fury fanbook. He ignored her after that.

That night there was a party, with all of Swank's band, most of Snuff Flix, a couple of guys from Cap Flash, and a general collection of friends and followers. Ken and Rick had gone off somewhere and got a good deal on a whole load of pills. Julie had got herself some acid, only her second ever trip, and she sat in a dark corner much of the evening looking bemused.

The two guys from Cap Flash were left pretty much to themselves. Captain Flash and the Instamatics started in the pub rock era, playing for the harder end of that market and getting themselves a good bit of local attention and notoriety as a result. But then punk rock exploded, all their younger fans started forming bands that were far harder than they could ever hope to be, and they found themselves increasingly a half-accepted, half-tolerated anachronism. You could always suss out the would-be poseurs when they started talking about how the Instamatics were their city's top New Wave band. They had just released an indie EP of good mid-seventies rock which had been played on Radio One but had yet to make a profit.

Rick was there with his girlfriend, Maureen. Their relationship was written all over her face. She constantly looked as if she had just been laid and had greatly enjoyed it. Rick was showing everyone some polaroid photos from that afternoon. He and Maureen had blown their profits from the gig on hiring a Rolls for an hour. The chauffeur had indulgently driven them around the streets while they waved enthusiastically at the pedestrians and looked out for friends, acquaintances, anyone at all that they could yell to.

Maureen was just getting into black magic and Aleister Crowley, whose name she could never pronounce. Rick was getting into it as well because he had the impression it had something to do with naked virgins on stone altars.

Out Of Reach was a better band than Snuff Flix even though they had not been together as long. Everyone said that. But Snuff Flix was still everyone's favourite. Swank's band was good, but Snuff Flix had Rick: Rick leaping on and off stage, Rick standing catatonically frozen while screaming his heart out, Rick falling about like a drunken epileptic then grabbing the mike just in time to yell the last verse and chorus. In real life Rick got on everyone's wick, all the time, but they flocked to see him perform.

John said, 'That girlfriend of his. He thinks everyone wants to fuck her. He won't let anyone near her.'

Derek said, 'I wouldn't want to fuck her. She looks like a slag.'

Swank's response to Rick's acclaim was to act bored. In fact, these days he seemed bored with everything. Julie was putting up the money for them to do an EP, but Swank's hopes for it wandered between total apathy and a grim determination. Tonight he was moody and uninterested, and Carrie did not know what to do with him. Except get horrendously drunk and make a lot of noise and try to shake him out of it. She was the centre of attention as soon as everyone got fed up with Rick's stupid photos, and Swank finally grinned and let her lead the way.

But before they left he had punched out some poor kid for no reason at all, so there was something going on inside him somewhere. Carrie always felt she fully understood Swank, but as soon as she tried to think out what to do about him she immediately lost whatever it was she had felt.

She let him wear himself out before she took him off home. His mood was even approaching mellow good humour by the time she got him into bed, and he was on top of her before she had got half her clothes off.

On the brick wall beneath the railway bridge, Mick, in large stiff letters, chalked the legend: JULIE – I LIKE FEELING YOUR TITS. And then he went over it in purple paint.

In the morning Carrie said, 'You realise Julie and Ken might be splitting up?'

Swank looked blank.

'Mick. From Snuff Flix,' Carrie said.

'Oh yeh?' He did not seem to attach any great importance to it. 'I'm not surprised really. I always wondered what she was doing with Ken.'

'And if that happens there's a good chance she'll leave our band and join Rick's.'

'Taking all her gear,' said Swank, disgusted, suddenly understanding. 'Ken's amp as well, 'cos she paid for that. And no EP. What about Snuff Flix's bass player, anyway?'

'I dunno. I think he's about ready for the push whatever happens. They're always giving him shit.'

'That's fucking good, innit?' He could see this band falling apart just like the last one. Another failure.

Carrie felt his frustrated anger, an anger that was turning in on itself, the foretaste of defeat as desolating as the real thing. She usually picked up his depressions, but then she held on to them even after his had cleared up so that he accused her of getting him down.

'Maybe she won't,' she said.

'I bet she will.'

They all turned up on Thursday evening to load the van up in good time for getting to the gig. It was at a church hall, like the one on the previous Friday, but it had been organised by George who, whatever his failings, generally knew what he was doing.

They were reluctantly blessed with the company of a local fanzine editor. He was a weedy youth in his late twenties and his dress was stylishly mock working class. He called his fanzine *National Collapse* and he had ambitions of writing for the *NME*. Swank got him busy carrying things into the van and then ignored him.

Instead Swank paid close attention, for the first time, to Julie and Ken.

'They don't look like anything's wrong between them,' he said to Carrie when they were all ready to go.

'There's not, as far as Ken knows.'

Swank shook his head. It was all beyond him.

In the van they interrogated the journalist. They'd never seen his fanzine before, and he said he had only done one issue. They asked him who was in it and he named some of the less interesting bands around. Carrie made a face, and he quickly justified himself by pointing out that it was his intention to cover the whole local scene.

'Like the *Yorkshire Post*, you mean?' Julie asked.

Swank suggested they do the interview right there in the van, blithely ignoring the effect on the audibility of the tape, and the journalist eagerly agreed. You could see him already writing the first paragraph in his head, all about how he had interviewed the band in the privileged discomfort of their private van.

He asked them about their politics.

Carrie suggested politics was a load of bollocks, Right or Left.

He understood this to mean they were doctrinaire anarchists seeking an anarchist State.

Swank pointed out that an anarchist State or an anarchist commune was not anarchy but just another political system, and the only sort of anarchy they were interested in was personal, individual anarchy.

He asked them if they did not think the violent overthrow of the State was the only legitimate means of political self-expression, this being wholly justified by the fascistic violence of the State against the people.

Swank fixed him with a measuring look.

'You read a lot, do you?' he asked, casually.

'Yes. Quite a bit, actually,' the journalist innocently replied, his voice tinged with intellectual pride.

'Thought so,' said Swank, to accompanying giggles.

They arrived at the hall just as the rain began. It was alone and unlit, the doors locked, and no sign of George or anyone else. The journalist was getting increasingly upset at their sardonic barbs, and was at the stage of loudly proclaiming his democratic right to express his own beliefs.

'There's a bus stop over there,' Swank told him. 'Should be one along in a few minutes.'

They walked all the way around the building but could find no way in short of breaking a window.

'Well, where's fucking George?' Julie demanded. 'He should be here with the key.'

They got back in the van and put on a tape to pass the time. The journalist, feeling himself unwanted, stayed outside, standing by the wall with his collar turned up against the damp, trying to look casual.

George finally arrived half an hour later, and told them the gig was off.

'The people who own the hall cancelled it just this morning. They said they hadn't realised it would be a punk band.'

They stood around him in an angry huddle.

'We had a booking, George,' pressed Swank. 'You gave them a deposit.'

'They gave it back to me,' George said, helplessly.

'But anyway,' he said, 'most of your crowd will be going to see that London band at the Railway Arms tonight, so even if we had gone ahead it's quite probable that not enough people would have turned up to make it worthwhile. I'm sorry. I did my best.'

He turned away regretfully while they took in the implication of collusion.

'Come on, let's go,' Swank said, wearily.

They climbed back into the van.

'Thanks for all your help, George,' Julie called.

Swank was thinking of how failed contenders always blamed others for their lack of talent, the pathetic way they tried to cover up mediocrity by attacking the middlemen. Feeling mediocre made him feel sick.

The journalist hurried up, anxious not to be left behind.

Swank rolled down the window.

'Fuck off,' he growled.

The van shot into the street.

They sat in silence, not really knowing what to do with themselves. A whole six hours was unexpectedly empty of activity. Outside it looked a pleasant sort of evening despite the rain. The lights were just beginning to be effective and as they got into the centre of town the streets were still full of people. Only they in their van were suddenly without purpose, and the bustle of others made it all the more obvious.

Then Julie was jumping to the door.

'Let me off here,' she said. 'There's Mick. He'll want to know I'm not playing tonight.'

Swank stopped the van.

'Hey!' yelled Ken, left behind, but she was already out in the street and closing the door.

'Bye!' she shouted, and hurried across the road.

Swank drove on.

On Saturday afternoon Swank and Carrie were sitting at home drinking tea when Julie turned up with Mick in tow. She sat down at the table and they offered her a drink. Mick remained standing, looking through their albums.

'So . . .' said Julie, not knowing how to start. 'What's happening?'

'So how's Ken?' asked Swank, tactful as ever.

Julie grinned.

Carrie brought over the tea. 'You're joining Snuff Flix, then?'

'Thing is,' said Julie, 'with splitting up with Ken it could be sort of difficult us both being in the same band.'

Swank raked his hand through his hair, then shrugged. 'Forget it,' he said. 'Doesn't matter.'

'Anyway, we were over at Ron's this morning collecting all my stuff, so it's all taken care of.'

'Fine,' said Swank.

Julie stirred her tea, still feeling embarrassed.

'So,' she said, picking up the cup. 'How are things going?'

KIM

There was once a young woman, darkly pretty, hired one blustery day in March to hand out tourist brochures in the Strand. They had done her up as a female beefeater, lurid and absurd in a skirt that stopped just short of her pubic hair and stuck out a full six inches all round on stiffened petticoats. She wore fishnet stockings with straight seams, her shoes were fastened with immense pink ribbons, and her arms and breasts were all but bare.

To complete the grotesqueness of the thing, the girl's dewy eyes and pink cheeks clearly showed that she had been wholly seduced by it all, that she truly believed herself transformed into the very essence of feminine gorgeosity. Once on TV there was a film of a rodeo, and she looked just like the monkeys that were tied to the backs of big dogs for the comic turn. While the dogs charged round and round the arena you were supposed to pretend the duped cowboys were fully aware of what was going on and were not just being taken for a ride.

It made Kim, down in London on holiday, think of what a girl at work had once said. When she was young the girl had always wanted to be named Georgina so people would call her George, or Roberta so she'd get Bob, or Andrea so she'd be Andy. If a real Robert went around wanting people to call him Dorothy people would think it very strange indeed. A fact which, Kim saw, said a great deal about what was what in the world.

Out of curiosity Kim went to a gay bar in Camden High Street which was supposedly noted for its drag shows. You went down a narrow passage beside the public bar to where there was a separate bar at the back. It was done up with carpets and wallpaper left over twenty years ago from someone's living-room, and on the wall were signed, framed photos of drag acts that had performed there. The male bar staff all had those Mrs Dale's Diary accents and that chubby awareness of their bodies that many homosexuals seem to develop.

Kim bought a drink and sat at a table near the stage.

Even though it was mid-week the place was soon full, every seat taken, and people standing wherever there was a little space. Directly in front of Kim sat two gay couples, that is, two girls together and two boys together. Young, normal, gentle. What impressed Kim was how often and how naturally the four touched as they talked, both across and within the sexes.

The famous performers that all these people had apparently come to see were two long-legged men dressed up in robes of diaphanous scarlet, mouthing to recordings of old-fashioned show tunes. They could probably have been mistaken for women at a distance. One of them opened his gown to reveal his tight black knickers, so that you were left wondering just what he had done with his bollocks. It was all trivially absurd. Never mind that a man dressed up as a woman looks like a cross between a faggot and a tart, it is sufficient wonder that he attempts such a thing at all. Kim left, feeling bemused and not at all attracted.

By the next afternoon his holiday was over, and he was back at King's Cross waiting for the train to the north.

On the way to the party, between the bus stop at the bottom of the street and the flats at the top, they passed a small dress shop with a violet silk evening gown in the window and a pair of delicate slippers.

And Mark, open mouthed, stopped to gaze at them in fascinated appreciation.

'Look at that dress,' he said.

'Oh fuck,' said Rick.

'Wow! I'd love to have a dress like that. And look at those shoes!'

Exchanged looks all round. They were long since accustomed to Mark. He never made any secret of his longings.

'Come on, Mark,' said Paul, taking hold of his arm and giving him a pull.

'I'd really love to have that dress,' Mark was still saying as they dragged him away.

'Then why don't you buy it?' asked Rick.

'No,' he said, sadly matter of fact. 'It wouldn't fit.'

They all unconsciously looked up to the top of Mark's head, half a foot above everyone else. It was true. With his long, ruler-thin figure it would be impossible to find a dress that looked good on him.

'All you need are a pair of tits,' said Rick. 'We could just cut off your balls and glue them on higher up.'

'There are really tall girls who look quite good,' said Paul.

'Yeh, I know,' Mark said, in a voice that showed he had by no means given up hope.

Kim said nothing.

Rob said, 'Are you, like, violently opposed to having sex with a woman? Like, does it make you feel sick?'

'No, it doesn't make me feel sick,' said Mark. 'It just doesn't turn me on, that's all.'

'He'd rather have sex with men,' said Rick, disgusted.

'Only as a girl, though. Only as a girl,' said Paul.

'Oh Rick!' Mark squealed, leaping about and grabbing hold of him. 'If I become a girl can I fuck you? Can I fuck you, Rick?'

'Get off!' yelled Rick. 'Get off! Get off!'

They all thought that was funny. No one who knew Mark was ever bothered by him. Whatever his inclinations, homosexual or bisexual or transsexual, in day-to-day life he was mostly asexual. And with his often unworldly air and the bizarre sounds he produced from the ever-changing, short-lived bands he put together he was also accepted as something of a genius, which made his peculiarities seem a little more natural.

Kim envied Mark. Kim was smaller, and he had a face and figure that were much more girlish. But he would never dare do the things Mark did, except perhaps if everyone knew it was only a joke.

At the party Mark said, 'I used to like Amanda Lear because I thought she was a transsexual, but then I found out she wasn't.'

Kim replied, carefully, 'I don't think I'd want a sex change unless I could end up looking like Marilyn Monroe.'

'Yeh,' said Mark. But the difference between Kim and Mark was that only Mark meant it. Could Kim have actually been reborn a girl he would not have been choosy about the ancillaries. But if Mark could not be Marilyn or Judy or Liza he was quite content just to fantasise about young boys.

Mark regularly took Paul to the pictures. While it was not actually known that anything more was going on, it was a fact that young Paul was growing softer and more feminine by the week.

Kim had been out with Mark a few times, but Mark had not found him pliable enough.

In the passage Maureen could be seen getting deeply involved with Rob. Kim had been out with Maureen a few times, as well. After three dates she had not even got as much as a goodnight kiss, and on the fourth date she didn't turn up.

Kim said, 'I suppose everyone is partially transsexual. That's why people get married, so that they can have both sides of themselves at once.' But Mark had not understood what he meant.

Kim got a job at a large Victorian hotel, looking after the stock cupboards that supplied the kitchens. Promotion, he was told, was inevitable should he prove suitable. But for now he pushed huge cartloads of foodstuff up and down lifts and along corridors, and ate lunch with the workers in the cafeteria. It was not an easy job for someone his size, but not impossible.

People laughed good naturedly as he struggled by with a load weighing sometimes up to 300 lb., and said things like, 'That'll put muscles on you,' and 'You'd better eat your vegetables.' He knew they expected him to be able to manage it, even if occasionally they gave him a hand. So manage it he did.

He imagined a girl trying to do it. Not impossible, but very different. He saw himself, with dark hair and flashing black eyes and the short, brown frock that the staff girls wore, trying to push the cart from the freight lift. He – she would give a half-hearted push, and then some kind, elderly man with greying hair and a twinkle in his eyes would say, 'That's a big load for a little girl,' and she would stand back and smile gratefully while he moved it for her. And in the regular management meeting on Thursday afternoon they would say, 'I really don't think Kim's strong enough to do that job. It was probably a mistake.' And someone else would say, 'Well there's an opening in the coffee shop now for a waitress.'

If Kim ever did seriously need help and there were only girls about, he knew it was no use asking them. They would not believe they could do it.

When he had started there, the first time he had delivered stuff to the classy bar on the ground floor and had not known where to put anything, a woman had walked in and then a man, and he had turned instinctively to the man, knowing he would be in charge. And he had glanced at the woman's face and seen she had perceived his thoughts.

Two weeks later he had seen one of the girls from the same bar sobbing loudly because she 'was not appreciated'. It occurred to him that there were reasons why the man was the boss.

It made his bizarre wishing all the more absurd and despicable.

At lunch he usually sat with some of the people from the kitchens. One day Jim sat down at their regular table, put his head down in his hands, and complained of being worn out.

'Too much poking?' asked Jack.

Malcolm came back from the machine with a cup of tea, singing a song that had been on the radio.

John said, 'If she's three times a lady, what does that make her?'

Jim looked up wearily. 'A slut,' he said.

They all laughed. Kim laughed with them.

At another table the women grouped and gossiped. The men ceased to talk of their usual interests when joined by women, and listened to the women's chatter in an attentive, kindly sort of manner, as if the women were children talking about toys.

It astounded Kim after the generally easy flow between the sexes at school. He was not used to hearing girls called things like Little Bo Peep. And he was not used to seeing that they liked it.

Malcolm put his cup on the table and sat down.

'Women are so fucking stupid,' he said, with sudden unexplained anger. 'So fucking stupid.'

There was a silent nodding of heads.

You often saw a man, emaciated and gawky, wandering about the centre of the city dressed in a ratty, black, fake fur coat and carrying a shiny plastic handbag. You would come across him unexpectedly at the bus stop or in a shop. He wore on his face an expression of wide-eyed vacancy meant to be feminine sensitivity, and on his chin he grew a straggling yellow beard, a scrawny goat's tuft, public testimony to his inner confusion. The stares he attracted were sometimes amused but mostly contemptuous. Only pure astonishment and his own timid caution saved him from being beaten up.

Kim said to himself, 'I'm not like that.' He said it deliberately and defiantly, almost out loud.

'That's not me.'

For a while Kim took a dance class, on Tuesday lunchtimes, in a large room behind a health food shop. It was a tiny class, never more than five or six, run by an unemployed blonde wanting to supplement her dole money. She tried to teach them jazz ballet while they discovered for the first time just how uncoordinated and stiff they were. Kim and a girl from Barclays Bank were the only regular students. The rest seldom lasted more than two weeks.

Kim was actually quite good at it, easily as agile as any girl. He was attracted to it not so much by the sensations of the dance as by the erotic images of clinging shiny leotards and tights. But on one wall was a floor-length mirror, some four feet wide, and Kim could not help being able to see himself as he danced. What he saw was so sharply at odds with what he wanted to imagine that finally he left.

He never even said more than hello to the girl from the bank, despite her interested looks.

Shortly after that Kim had a week's holiday, seeing the real world on a weekday morning for the first time in far too long. He took the bus into town on the Monday morning and wandered about as whim suggested with nothing much to do and a deliberately empty wallet, grateful for his temporary freedom. The streets were emptier, the kids were in school, most of the men were in their offices or factories.

The women, it seemed to Kim, enjoyed this sort of freedom all of the time. If he had been at work he would have just finished his tea-break with a full six and a half hours to get through before he could call his time his own. These young wives, however, could browse around the shops for as long as they wanted, and go home when it pleased them. In the afternoon a friend from two doors down would come over and they would have a comfortable talk and a cup of tea until the kids came home, noisy and cheerful, demanding and pleasing. It seemed a much better life than supplying Jim and Malcolm with 50 lb. sacks of onions.

He turned off the main streets into the rows of tall terraced houses and corner shops. There were younger mothers here, tireder and untidier mothers with pre-school toddlers in tow. A heavy child she had to carry, a youngster that whined irritably and made her sharp and resentful or that chattered bright streams of talk that she no longer listened to.

There was a commotion going on down a side street: Swank and Carrie locked in a ferocious row. Swank would grab Carrie by the hair and swing her around so that both her feet left the ground, and Carrie would scream and curse and beg. She looked as if she was trying to run away, but once she was loose there was nc retreat. Now it was Swank who had to guard his head and his shins, till he could grab her by the waist and hurl her bodily across the street. People walked by trying not to notice. Cars sounded their horns and manoeuvred around them.

She threw an empty Coke can at him, then half a brick, and when he ducked his head she tackled him like a rugby player and brought them both to the ground. And then she was astride him and would have clawed his face open if he had not grabbed her by both wrists and twisted her off him into the dirt. She was up before he was, but she was not quick enough to prevent him grabbing her arm and twisting it up behind her back so that she could not struggle without causing herself more pain. He marched her back into the house, her face contorted with fury. You could see he wanted nothing better than to give her a good kicking. Soon their yells began to float out of their second floor window.

Kim walked away.

Every day at four o'clock the day shift hung up their work clothes and signed themselves out and the night shift put on their work clothes and signed themselves in. The housekeeper, in nominal command over their comings and goings, had her office beside the women's cloakroom in the basement, just behind Kim's storeroom. For twenty minutes every night there was banging of doors and running of feet and loud laughter and shouting down the corridor, and over it all the housekeeper, a great rock solid woman with a permanent ache, stampeded shrilly about, imposing order and discipline. Then there was a gradual quietening, and at 4.30 p.m. the housekeeper put on her own coat, locked up her office, and went home to help her husband into an early grave.

Kim, on his own schedule that did not set him free till five, was left with half the basement to himself. With all his work done, all the night supplies delivered, he had nothing to do but some trivial tidying up.

One afternoon, with even that completed and twenty minutes to spare, wandering about with nothing to do, he tried the door to the women's cloakroom and, finding it unlocked, he slipped cautiously inside. It was small and poorly lit. There was a fat, comfortable-looking bed down one wall, a tattered romance novel beneath a chair, and a reproduction of the eighteenth-century countryside on the wall. The men's changing room had only metal chairs, and the management periodically cleared the wall of pin-ups.

Along one side of the room was a rack on which the day-shift waitresses had hung their frocks, short puffed sleeves, lace around the neck, cut low and square so that when one bent over to take an order she displayed a good acreage of bosom. Kim touched them.

He returned to the storeroom and put on his coat. He came back to the cloakroom, grabbed a dress from the rack and bundled it up beneath his coat, then fled back to his storeroom. He was certain someone must have seen him, someone watching from a nook or hidden in the shadows. He put the dress on under his shirt, tucked it into his trousers, put his coat back on, and went home.

As long as he had not been seen, as long as no one came to him tomorrow and demanded what he knew of the disappearance of a waitress's dress, then it could not have been easier.

As soon as he was home he closed the curtains, stripped naked and put the dress on over his head, and with some difficulty fastened the buttons up the back. He put his hands in the large pockets at the front. It fitted him well, purely by good fortune. But the skirt seemed too wide, and somehow graceless. He was surprised by how coarse the material was. It did not feel good between his fingers and it made his skin feel prickly. He took a few experimental steps. He was disappointed by how unsensual and purely functional the dress actually was. After a few minutes you would completely forget you were wearing it. Only a serious effort of self-delusion would make it seem otherwise.

He stuffed some socks down the sagging empty space where his breasts should have been, then pulled them out in disgust. He felt embarrassed by the dainty lace and the cutesy sleeves. He went to look in the mirror, hoping, standing on a chair so that he could see how the dress looked on him.

He looked like a man in a dress. Hipless, thick waisted with trunk-like unclothed legs. The dress conferred no glamour of womanhood.

He put the chair away, then came back to study his face. It was not so bad. Plain perhaps, made even plainer by the frilly lace, but not ugly. A little make-up, a wig, earrings, a necklace. Stockings to disguise his legs. A loose coat to hide his figure. Only go out at night.

He felt depressed.

Two days later he put the dress in a plastic bag from Woolworth's and left it in a vacant lot behind a factory.

He just wished he could see some point in any of this.

THE THIEF

Down on the Strand among the gaslights and the drizzle and the hansom cabs of the theatre-goers, Carrie in a shortened skirt displayed her wares for the men and kept an eye and a half open for the police.

A young man from the provinces in his best suit – good in cloth, dated in style, ugly in cut – gawking at the confusion, ogling the women in their furs and satins. He catches a glimpse of her ankles, moving up over her uncorseted waist and breasts and her painted eyes.

She gives him a wink.

He stops and stares.

She gives him a nod, and half a blown kiss.

He approaches.

'Hey, er, Miss. You aren't one of them . . . one of them *girls* are you?'

Young, inexperienced, excitable. She took his arm in a firm but friendly grip, smiled comfortingly and promisingly, and led him into an alley.

'I haven't got a lot of money, but we don't need too much of that to have a bit of fun, eh? How much do you charge? I've heard all about girls like you. I bet you're even worth a bonus, eh?'

She stood him before the arch of a doorway, both her hands on his collar, and brought him forward to kiss him.

A hand came out of the dark and placed itself around his neck and squeezed. He gasped and snorted and struggled and kicked.

'Stay still, yokel,' said Swank, 'or I'll squeeze the life out of you.'

Carrie was already at the man's pockets, removing quietly and efficiently a watch, a wallet, a pen, a silk handkerchief, and some coins. The man's eyes were bulging and frightened. She put the things in a big pocket in her skirt, and patted his face, lovingly.

'All right,' she said to Swank.

Swank gave a final squeeze so that the man's tongue stuck out, and Carrie raised her skirt with both hands and kneed him in the groin. They left him on the ground and ran up the alley, up the steps into Maiden Lane, and were soon far away among the hidden streets.

They halted in another doorway when they thought they were sufficiently distant from the scene of the crime, and counted the coins.

'Seven and thruppence farthing,' she said.

'And the wallet.'

She looked.

'Two pounds.'

'And with the watch and the kerchief, that's a good haul.'

They had stayed this side of Charing Cross, and now they turned north, along narrow unlit streets, full of eyes that glanced at them then glanced away, for they so clearly belonged that they did not arouse suspicion.

They turned into a small yard at the end of which stood the Queen's Teeth, yellow and displaced with age, in gums of cobble and spittle of mud and horseshit. They went through the little door into the light.

The place was smoky but no more than comfortably full. They found a small table to themselves and the serving girl came for their order. They wanted hot brandy with spices.

'Moving up in the world, are we?' asked the serving girl, who had seen them in when they could barely afford mugs of water.

Swank leered. 'Just the beginning, darling.' And he put his hand out to pinch her bottom, but she had moved away.

'Come on, Swank, I'm hungry, stop fooling about,' Carrie scowled. Her stomach was beginning to anticipate hot food after a long fast. 'When was the last time we had a decent meal? Long enough, anyway.'

'Too long.' The serving girl was back with their drinks. 'We

'Well?' he said.

'We've got some stuff. A watch and things.'

He drew on his pipe, not looking at them.

'I'm not a fence, you know.'

'I was thinking you could give them to your . . . friends, and take a cut, seeing as I don't know anyone in these parts yet. I was thinking perhaps you could put some work my way.'

Mr Jack indulged himself in thought.

'Let's see them,' he said at last.

Swank nodded to Carrie, and she spread the goods on the table. It suddenly did not seem like very much.

Mr Jack picked up the wallet and looked inside.

'I give twelve and six on the pound for notes,' he said.

It was far less than they had hoped.

'Take it or leave it. No shop will take notes from the likes of you.'

Swank nodded.

Mr Jack signalled one of his henchmen, who took out a bag and counted out twenty-five shillings, and pushed them across the table to Swank. Swank pushed them to Carrie, who swept them all into her best purse.

'And the rest?'

'We'll see.'

It was not at all satisfactory, but it was best to leave it for the moment. Certainly they had no immediate way of getting rid of it all themselves.

Mr Jack drew on his pipe.

'You're from the north,' he said.

'Yeh. Yorkshire.'

He nodded. 'How long in London?'

'About a week.'

'Finding all the opportunities and riches you expected? Lots of gold lying about in the street, that sort of thing?'

The henchmen eyed each other and shook their heads. Swank felt he was being laughed at.

'We're doing all right.'

'Hmmph,' said Mr Jack.

'Like I said, if you could put something our way. We know our job.'

Mr Jack again surveyed the few goods on the table. 'This is all you have to show for a week's work?'

'Well it takes a bit of time to adjust to how things are done down here and get accustomed to things. Up in Yorkshire we knew everyone and it was a lot easier. It's just we don't really know anyone yet. When we've found our feet we'll do better than this.'

Mr Jack drew on his pipe.

'Mary . . .' he indicated the serving girl. 'Mary will have your money the day after tomorrow.'

They were being dismissed.

'And can you put something our way?' Swank was reluctant to leave without some assurance.

'We'll see.'

The two henchmen began to study them pointedly, and so, feeling uneasy, Swank and Carrie got up from the table and left. The men stared after them. Mr Jack returned to his pipe.

'You're not going to take them on are you?' said one.

Mr Jack sniffed. 'Yokels,' he said, and the pair chuckled.

Outside the drizzle had stopped but the air smelt oddly, as if someone was burying something or cutting up bad meat. There was a woman on the corner, young, strangely well-dressed for these streets, although with a ragged shawl around her as if by way of disguise. She stopped them as they passed, looking over Carrie's clothes, her hand on Carrie's arm.

'Are you a whore?' she asked. She pronounced it who-er.

'No I'm not!' retorted Carrie indignantly.

She received a sudden cuff about the head from Swank, and said in a quieter voice, 'What of it?'

The woman looked down at the ground.

'Can you come to my house tomorrow?' she said.

Carrie looked swiftly at Swank, but his face told her that if there was money to be made here she had better make it.

'What's all this about then?' she asked.

'Can you . . . Will you . . .' The woman took a card from inside her sleeve. There was no name on it, only an address.

'Come in through the area. Ask for the Mistress. Tell them you're a seamstress or something.'

'Yeh, all right.' Carrie put the card in her pocket.

'Tomorrow morning, at ten o'clock.' The woman looked full at her then, an intense stare. Carrie nodded, feeling only wonder.

The woman said nothing more, but walked quickly away from them, down the way they had just come.

'Well,' said Carrie. 'Imagine that. Stupid bitch. Do you think her lame, blind husband has got a taste for honest working girls, or do you think Madame is just too shy to go looking for upper-class dykes?'

'You'll go,' said Swank.

She knew he meant it. She knew how he had felt when Mr Jack had asked them if the yokel's goods were all they had to show for themselves.

'Couldn't we just get a good look at the place and rob it?'

'We'll do that too.'

'The sow.'

They reached home within ten minutes. Home was a tiny shack made of old doors and charred beams and worn carpeting, along with half a dozen similar shacks on a patch of burnt rubble where two weeks ago had been a rotting, bug-infested hovel. They had grabbed this tiny unsanitary corner in preference to the dismal hell they had occupied on their first two nights in London, a damp basement room shared with five other couples which, with a few crusts of bread, had cost them the last of their money.

Carrie lived in fear that they would come back one day and find someone had stolen even this meagre home from them.

Back in Yorkshire they had had a furnished room with a water tap in the yard almost right outside their door.

They flopped down on the rough surface and wrapped themselves in the blankets they had stolen from a pawnbroker.

Carrie felt Swank's hand at her clothes.

'Oh God, Swank. Not tonight.'

'Cow,' said Swank, and took her anyway.

They awoke cold and tired, bones aching, with the first light. There was no food for breakfast, but at least now there was money to buy some.

'I'm going to set fire to this place when we get a new one,' Carrie said. She stood miserably in the middle of the floor, a blanket wrapped around her clothes, while Swank fastened up his laces. He put on his long coat.

'Come on,' he said.

The cold was only in the shadows. The sky was flawless and the world looked beautiful. Even in these streets it was beautiful. Blue-black shadows where people were smudged, a sharp dividing line, then golden brick and cement, glowing streets, even a dazzling marmalade cat that darted away into an impossibly small opening.

Breakfast was a tuppenny carton from the winkle man in Dudley Street, eaten with dirty fingers, strolling and talking, beginning to relax again. It was like a holiday. It was as if a few shillings in your pocket made you a person of leisure who could saunter about in the early morning sun and enjoy the picturesque ugliness of the city – which they had hardly seen until now, being so caught up with worry and chaos and not knowing what to do – as if it had been created specially for your benefit.

They wandered through the narrow streets until their way began to be blocked by baskets and boxes and crates and cartons, and the streets were full of carriages and drays, and the pavements filled with fruiterers and farmers and maids and cooks, voices and wagon wheels, loud and soft and squealing and rumbling, and they were in Covent Garden. There they bought the rest of their breakfast, aided by Carrie's good eye for quality and a bargain, better and sharper than any kitchen maid still half full of sleep, because she had known what it was to make a shilling worthwhile, and make a penny last, and steal when there was neither.

And Swank nodded from time to time and looked surly when Carrie had to haggle, and quietly accepted all she gave him.

They ate in the streets again, among the clerks going to their offices and the working men already going about their jobs. Quietly and contentedly sucking on their fingers and depositing the core and peel in the gutter.

'It's a start,' said Carrie. 'We're human again. We're not hungry animals no more. And we've still got a good thirty shillings. How long will that last us? A month if it has to. Lots of time.'

And Swank looked up at the clock on St Martin's and said, 'You've got to be in Hyde Park Square in an hour and a half,' and the holiday was over.

'Damn,' said Carrie. She took a last bite on a pear and threw away the remains. She wiped her fingers on her dress. 'I don't think I want to go there,' she said.

Swank grunted and strode off ahead of her so that she had to half run to keep up.

'Well it doesn't make any sense, Swank, does it? What's she want wandering about in the streets like that for? What does she think she's doing, anyway?' But Swank was clearly not interested.

'Well what if it's, if it's, white slavers or something or, or, devil worshippers? It can't be anything normal if she has to go looking for women in the street like that. Swank?'

Swank said, 'What I want from you is the details of the place and the best way for us to rob it.'

And that was an end to it.

'And while you're gone I'll find us a new place to live. All right?'

Carrie looked discontented.

'Sow,' she said.

When she had put on the best of her two dresses and had gone, Swank went first to the Queen's Teeth because he was known there, then followed a trail of leads and advice, liberally distributing pennies and thruppenny bits to keep it warm, and by noon had secured them an attic flat in Duke's Passage. It had only a skylight for illumination, but it had a sloped ceiling, which appealed to him, and surprisingly it occupied the whole attic floor, which meant he could lock the door at the bottom of the stairs as well as to the room. It would be a long walk for water, though. And a long haul with coal. And with furniture.

He went from there back to their shack, and found Carrie already waiting for him, looking sullen.

'How'd it go?' he said.

'The bitch wouldn't let me in. I never even got past the kitchen door.'

'Not get . . .'

'First there's a maid who stands there gawping and don't knowing, and then she calls Cook who looks at me as if I'm something she'd thrown out with the chamber pots, and I show her the card and tell her the Mistress wanted to see me at ten, and that I was a seamstress about the Mistress's new dress, and she just says, "Are you now?" And I says, "Well send upstairs and ask the Mistress herself because you're going to get into right trouble if you send me away because I was specifically told that I was to come here today at ten o'clock, and that was your Mistress's orders to my Mistress." So finally she does send up, and comes back looking all evil and triumphant and says Mistress has never heard of me and was expecting no such caller.

'So then I come on all faint and have to be carried into the house, seeing as how they couldn't really leave me on the doorstep. But they don't even give me a cup of water, and the minute I've got my eyes open and am beginning to think about sitting up they chuck me out again.'

'So you didn't see anything.'

'Nothing of any use. There's a young kitchen maid called Sarah who looks overworked and unhappy enough. You could always see if you could do something with her.'

It was something to go on, anyway.

He told her about the flat, and she was cheerful again. Moving took only the time needed to divide their possessions in two, pick them up, and walk the short distance to Duke's Passage.

'It's not very light, is it?' she said, looking about.

'It's not bad,' said Swank.

'No, I suppose not. I was just saying . . .'

'It's lighter earlier on. It gets the morning sun.'

'Oh . . .'

She studied the fireplace.

'I hope that chimney's not blocked.'

Swank grunted a sigh and headed for the door.

'Where are you going?'

'Out,' said Swank. 'I've got to think.'

Swank wandered aimlessly about the streets, not really thinking, just enjoying the warmth of the sun, waiting for a course of action to suggest itself. Lunch was a pie and a drink in a pub, then back on the streets again. So many people knew him back home, people of his kind, friends, people in the same line of work, but here nobody glanced at him twice. It was refreshing.

He wouldn't go over to Hyde Park Square just yet. It didn't do to have too many strangers coming around at once. Little Sarah would keep for a couple of days.

He passed a commotion of some sort coming from a yard, and turned in to have a look.

It seemed as if some men, two men, were abusing some girl, shouting at her and slapping her about the face. And whatever the cause of it, the people watching from windows and from doorways seemed to think her the source of the trouble, for they jeered at her and shouted encouragement to the men.

Swank stopped to watch, as did others from the street, so that a small crowd began to form.

He could not hear what the girl was screaming, but one of the men was calling her a pig, over and over again, and slapping her head hard with his open hands, so that she staggered about as if she was drunk. Although she might have been drunk as well.

Then the other man grabbed at her dress and pulled so that it came away at the waist and was hanging on only a quarter of the way around, and everyone cheered and cackled and shouted. And the girl started to scream all the more, and you could see at the tear that she was not wearing anything underneath it, so that when the two men both seized on it and tore it off completely she was naked from the waist down.

If she had had time she might have stopped awkwardly and tried to cover herself, or more usefully she might have looked for some weapon to fight back with, some loose cobblestone to smash at their heads. But they were on her so fast that all she did was go down heavily with a boompf of air, and one of the men already had his trousers down, to cheers and whistles from the women, while the other had one hand trying to undo his buttons and the other hand trying to get at her breasts.

And then there were two policemen pushing their way calmly through the mob, and the cheers became jeers and insults. The men stopped when they saw the police, and stood up rather shame-faced and began rearranging their clothes. One of the policemen tried to help the girl get up, but she spat at him, and twisted around to her feet with the agility of some beautiful animal, and ran off naked down a narrow passageway.

The shouts became louder, and a woman at a window threw a piece of broken crockery that shattered on the ground at the policeman's foot. The cries became laughter and taunts. Someone threw a stone. Someone threw a small log. Then a bigger stone. The policemen began to force their way out of the yard. One of them had his hat knocked off. The other had his nose bloodied. They blew on their whistles for assistance, and swung out with their truncheons.

Once they had made their escape things calmed down a bit and there was no more shouting. But the crowd hung about, excited, wanting something else to happen. A youth threw a stone at a window, just to let off energy, and broke it. An old man in a night cap stuck his head out angrily, but saw the grinning mob beneath him and quickly withdrew.

'All right, young'un. None of that,' said a beefy, red-faced man, and clipped the youth's ear.

Then the police were back, six of them in a bunch at the end of the street. The crowd had a target and a purpose again. The air was once more filled with jeers and shouting. Swank saw that the people around him were looking tense and expectant, as if they were about to enjoy themselves at something very serious.

One policeman, in a different hat from the rest, overturned a wooden box to stand on it, and read from a sheet of paper that anyone who did not disperse within ten minutes would be arrested and charged under the Riot Act.

More jeers.

A closed wagon could be seen drawing up at the corner, its back door opened, and a dozen more policemen got out.

A thrill of nerves ran through the crowd as they realised this was for real. People began to pick up stones to throw.

The shouting grew louder. The first six policemen stepped back a few yards to join their comrades. The one who had spoken surveyed the mob with his hands in his belt, as if he was a general and they were his army.

A bottle sailed through the air and splintered beside him. Then a large cobblestone, freshly torn from the ground. Then a dozen smaller stones, and the battle was on.

Swank was in the middle of it. He picked up stones and threw them. He smashed crates and swung out with the pieces. He smashed a shop window and he smashed the glass in a pub doorway. He was within striking distance of a policeman, but missed. Sometimes he could hardly keep his feet. He was pulled and jostled and ran with the mob because he could do nothing else – and wanted to do nothing else. There was no order, no charges and counter-charges, no waiting in doorways to see what would happen next, then a rush down the street with a volley of missiles, then a rush back as the police charged. Just an unholy fearsome blood-raising fist-swinging exhilarating destructive mêlée.

The whole battle swept right up the street, police and all, taking with it anything and anyone that either did not or could not get out of the way. At the corner it broadened out into the crossroads, the mob losing its density to the other streets, and Swank was pressed with a small group up the side road in a disorganised tumble of bodies until they spilled out, blinking and bewildered, into the sunlight and the astounded shoppers on Oxford Street.

Swank shook himself and turned a quick right. He darted into a shop, and stood absorbed by the leather spines of some incomprehensible books, tugging his clothes back into a semblance of neatness.

People, well-dressed respectable people, were looking at him. A young assistant was approaching with the supercilious air of the paid middle-class bully. Swank smoothed back his hair with both his hands as he looked the assistant full in the eye. Then he turned and left at a calm and leisurely pace, closing the door gently behind him.

There was no sign of trouble, neither rioters nor police. He walked back the way he had come and looked down the street he had been shot from. A stout policeman regarded him thoughtfully, but there were no other indications of any disturbance. No doubt somewhere there were a few cracked heads, recovering in a friendly snug or a pitiless jail, but the main event seemed to have blown over as quickly as it had started.

Anyway, he would not hear from Mr Jack until tomorrow, and he could not really start on Mistress Sarah until at least the day after that. So he might as well go back to the attic, and tonight he and Carrie might as well go out and enjoy themselves.

Which is exactly what they did.

By ten they were back at the Queen's Teeth and Swank had a taste for cider. But instead of taking their orders, Mary, the serving girl, threw a small bag on the table, a bag that clinked as with muffled money.

'It's from Mr Jack,' she said.

Swank looked surprised and relieved. He flashed a quick grin at Carrie, then turned back to Mary. 'Great. What are you drinking?'

'Aren't you going to open it?' asked Mary.

Swank glanced at Carrie. She was frowning at something in the middle distance that did not seem to exist. He felt vaguely irritated by her. He pulled the cord and spilled the coins out on the table. There did not seem to be many. He smoothed them out to count them.

'Is that all?'

'That's the lot. Mr Jack says the stuff wasn't worth much, and he has to make something on the deal himself.'

'Yeh, well . . .' Swank was uncertain. He knew how powerless he was in this strange city, all his friends and allies two hundred miles away. For the moment, at least, it was Mr Jack's game.

'When can we see Mr Jack?'

Carrie noticed two men at another table, staring at them quite openly, laughing. She stared back at them, but they did not look away. She turned her attention to Swank to avoid seeming to be outstared.

'Mr Jack doesn't want to see you,' Mary was saying. 'Not till you've got something worthwhile for him.'

'But we were hoping – that is, I was under the impression that Mr Jack was going to put something our way.'

'Well,' said Mary, 'you was wrong, wasn't you?'

Others were watching and listening. Carrie could feel them.

Mary said, 'And Mr Jack says he doesn't want you in here every night bothering him. So you'll have to leave.'

Swank looked stunned. Carrie grabbed his hand as he lurched to his feet, and he recovered himself in time to notice the silence and the alert look to the men who just seconds ago had been quietly drinking.

'Go on,' said Mary, with a sideways nod towards the door. 'Hop it.'

Swank scowled, and still holding Carrie's hand marched towards the street.

'Goodbye, Yorkshire,' called a quiet voice, and there was muttered laughter.

'Too big for himself, that one,' someone said, as the door slammed and the men went back to drinking.

Swank marched down the street, lips tight, eyes looking straight ahead, Carrie chasing after him, silent and afraid. People got out of their way.

It's not my fault, Carrie whispered to herself. It's not my fault. I've done my best, too, Swank, just like you have.

'Let's go home, Swank. Let's go to bed. We'll be able to think better in the morning. We don't need bastards like him. Ugly scarred drooling bastard. We've always managed without their kind before. We've always survived before, we'll survive now. I know we will. Come on, Swank.'

'What happens if someone from back home comes down to see how we're getting on and expecting us to be doing good and be able to fit them up with lodgings and connections, like we said we would? What then?'

They were only a little way from Trafalgar Square, and Swank had finally slowed down. Carrie said nothing. They're not going to expect all that after just one week, she thought, reasonably.

'Swank, let's go home,' she said. She took his arm and he shook her off. Then he relented and put his arm around her shoulder, and she leaned her head against him, the roughness of his coat feeling familiar and comforting. They turned into the Square, beneath the aloof indifference of the National Gallery.

'We'll get something together,' Carrie said, to his buttons.

'Mugging? Garrotting? Whoring? We haven't had to rob people in the streets since we were kids, Carrie.'

Carrie sniffed, and raised her head, trying to think.

'Well what about the docks? You always said there was lots of money to be made in the docks.'

'But we don't know anybody there either, do we? Are we just supposed to follow the wagons as they come up from the quay, compete with the kids for whatever's loose, and sell it for pennies at some Jewish pawnshop?'

'But we've got to start somewhere,' said Carrie. But she did not want to do that, either. And she got no enjoyment out of garrotting yokels. And she would not go back to whoring, never.

'Anyway,' she said, 'we've still got a good bit of money left, with what we got tonight.'

'We've not go so very much money, either,' said Swank. 'I spent most of that ten bob you gave me on looking for a room and God knows what else. Seeing as how we were expecting so much more.'

They walked in gloomy silence until Carrie could stand it no more.

'Oh Christ, Swank!' she burst out. 'We're good. We're bloody professionals. I bet we can take anything we want in this city. We can get stuff so good the connections will come looking for *us*. And that sow's whelp, Mr Jack, will come sniffing after us too. And when he does, I'll scar the other side of his face.'

'Yeh, I know,' said Swank, quietly. 'It's just that it saps your confidence, everything being so confusing and new. It's like you're drowning. You keep looking out for things to hold on to when you should be trying to swim.'

'Yeh,' said Carrie, more gently.

'Let's go home, Swank.'

They turned off the Square into the little streets behind the Haymarket and Lower Regent Street. It was darker here, and no one about except for a man stumbling towards them in an odd, disturbing manner, as if he was overly drunk.

'Some lord out slumming by the looks of him,' said Swank.

'He's been worked over too. Look at the state of his clothes,' Carrie said, as they approached.

The man saw them, and stood almost erect, swaying. Even in this light they could see the bruises on his face, and the rips in his clothing.

'Please,' he said, his voice slurred. 'I've been robbed. Hooligans. Murderers. They beat me up.'

'And why'd they do that, now?' asked Swank, sounding malicious and dangerous.

'I don't know. I wasn't doing any harm. I . . .'

'He's been out whoring,' said Carrie. 'See, he's got the look of a lecher about him. Won't your rich women have you, that you have to come molesting the poor?'

'Now look,' said the man, beginning to feel afraid all over again. 'Now look.'

'Molesting poor girls, was he?' said Swank. 'Why, you obscene old bastard. You disgusting piece of gold-plated, satin-cushioned crap. You make me ashamed, you do. And we're supposed to look up to your sort. You make me ashamed of the whole snivelling human race.'

The man was backed against the wall, holding up his hands, trembling, looking for a means of escape.

'Go on, Swank,' said Carrie. 'Sort him out.'

And Swank hit him and hit him again, fist against soft flesh, fist against hard bone, fist against slippery wet skin. And Carrie joined in with her own fists and with her own feet, and the man was down between them on the ground, and he only cried out once, just before the last kick that knocked him unconscious.

'Come on,' they said, and they ran away down the murky streets until they were well clear of the crime.

And there in the dark they stopped and breathed hard and stared at each other, and wiped their foreheads with their hands and wiped their mouths with their sleeves, and laughed at each other, and felt better.

MORE LIFE

Monday night Herbert came down from the flat upstairs (they lived on the ground floor of an old house in Notting Hill now), cradling a huge female tabby. The tabby purred.

'What's this one called?' Carrie asked, making her voice apologise for her ignorance.

'This is Sophia,' said Herbert, his voice adding the 'of course' she had expected.

Sophia meowed, and struggled to be released. She dropped to the floor and began her exploration, hiding her curiosity as best she could beneath her dignity, tail twitching.

'How many have you got now?' Carrie asked.

'Forty-three,' said Herbert, without thinking. 'Alexander died, but Martinique had kittens.'

'Fancy a Guinness, Herbert?' said Swank, bringing in three bottles from the little kitchen. He propped himself up against the battered sideboard. 'I dunno how you manage with all those fucking cats.'

Herbert was muddy-haired, rough-skinned and of uncertain age. He had eyes that seemed to stare, disconcerting till you knew him, because company made him so very nervous. It had taken months of overt acceptance of him before he had begun to feel safe enough to visit Swank and Carrie. Other than those visits they saw Herbert only on his regular trips down to the supermarket, in smelly clothes and an overly long, greasy coat, to spend his benefit money on mountains of cat food.

'People don't understand cats,' said Herbert. 'I mean, suppose a kitten shits on the table, most people would hit it. But you shouldn't do that. It's up to the older cats to teach it the proper way to do things. You've got to respect cats.'

'A girl at work says her cat's turning into a homosexual,' said Carrie. 'She caught him trying to bugger their neighbour's tom.'

Swank grinned to himself, but Herbert accepted her words as seriously as she had spoken them.

'Sex isn't the same for cats,' he said, and they settled down to a dissertation on his observations of cat sexuality, while Sophia, uninterested, sharpened her claws on the legs of the charity shop coffee table. Herbert spoke always in long monologues, piecing together for a rare audience thoughts he had shared so far only with his cats.

'The thing is,' he said, finally, 'people think I'm strange because I've got so many cats, but the thing is, I chose to live this way and I accepted all the consequences. And that's what you've got to do. Like, a cat doesn't stop and worry about what people will think. A cat decides what it's going to do and then it does it, as best it can. Like, I've learnt a lot from cats. People have got to learn and grow, and I live in the way I choose so that I can grow in the way I choose, and so that it's up to me, not anyone else, how I am.'

And his eyes stared wider and his face became whiter as he demanded yet again that they understand him and appreciate him.

'Actually,' said Swank, beginning to get seriously interested despite himself, 'I know just what you mean.' And Herbert's face became almost normal again.

'I'd better be getting back up there,' he said. 'See what they're up to. Sophie.' He made for the door, with Sophia bounding after him.

'See you, Herbert,' Carrie said, following him to the door, although he was halfway up the stairs by now. 'Call in again.'

Tuesday morning and Victor, Carrie's supervisor at work, was in a temper.

Fucking Victor. Shut up.

She switched off the kettle and sat down with her coffee and newspaper. It was 8.45.

Victor was in a temper over three things. The post-boy was on holiday and Victor had been delegated to take the meter to the post office to get it topped up. The meter was quite a small thing to look at, but by the time you had reached the bottom of the street your arm was certain it was solid steel throughout, and the women from Accounts who were looking after the letters for the week refused to touch it. Victor was tall and thin and over-educated. He did not see why fate had thrown him down here instead of easing him into academia where he belonged. When something needed to be done Victor was first to volunteer but when the time came to actually do the work he would fume at the imposition, and doubly so this time of morning when he was accustomed to sitting in his office reading up government reports and the more serious sections of the *Guardian*. So that was the first thing.

He had not even returned the meter to the mail-room when he noticed the state of the passage. Carrie heard him stamp down the stairs to the caretaker's home in the basement. Then there was a pause, then a heavy clattering, and she knew he was bringing up the mop and pail. He went through this performance quite regularly, at least twice a week. The cleaners were his demons, his mother-in-law, his British Rail. If he could not find something, the cleaners must have taken it, he was always getting his fingers black on dust the cleaners had left behind, not once had the cleaners done the passage floor properly. She heard the water go swooshing over the lino, then the shocked bangs of the mop and Victor's muttered fury. It would all have made Carrie quite dizzy if she had allowed herself to think about it.

'Good morning workers!' It was Rawlings, the head of the department, coming in from the street. 'Oh.' Seeing only Carrie. 'Where's Victor?'

'I dunno,' mumbled Carrie, not looking up.

Victor could be heard quite plainly out in the passage.

Rawlings put down the little paper bag he was carrying and pulled out two styrofoam cups of coffee from the shop next door, his regular morning supply. He took the top off one of them and tried a cautious sip.

'I don't know how anyone can drink this stuff,' he said, as he did every morning. He rummaged in the bag again and pulled out a large cream bun, his first of the day.

Rawlings was large and fat and looked as if he was made of

hamburger. When Carrie was eating she could not bear to have to look at him. He was about to stuff the cream bun in his mouth when he noticed the rumpus in the passage. He opened the door.

'There's Victor!' he said.

Carrie made some effort to look appropriately surprised.

Victor hastened back into the office, still clutching the mop. 'I've had enough of this,' he said, speaking with barely repressed rage. 'I've had just about enough.'

'It's terrible,' said Rawlings. 'I don't know what's wrong with them.'

'Well I've had just about enough!' He disappeared into his private office.

'I've got you some coffee, Victor,' Rawlings called, just as he did every morning. He picked it up and followed Victor into the office. 'I don't know how anyone can drink this stuff.'

Carrie stuck up an offensive finger behind his back, then folded up the paper in disgust.

So that was the second thing.

And then in the post was the news that the printer who supplied the forms on which customers wrote out their classified ads was moving his office so the records would have to be altered and there would be a new telephone number and they would have to send a memo to Accounts. It was five minutes' work at most, but Victor was crackling with indignation.

'What are we supposed to do?' he demanded. 'Do they think we've got nothing else to worry about but changing peoples' addresses all day?'

'You just do as best you can,' said Rawlings, in full sympathy with him. 'If we haven't got the time to deal with it they'll just have to wait. First things first. There's only twenty-four hours in a day.'

Carrie idly cleaned her nails with the end of a letter opener. They had been out of the forms for two months and she had been duplicating them fifty at a time. She could have ordered new ones herself by simply picking up the phone, but Victor had refused to allow it and had said he would do it. A week ago she had wondered when they were going to arrive. Victor had looked annoyed, then said he would get them ordered tomorrow.

So that was the third thing, and apart from Victor unlocking the doors it was a day like any other, without even the anticipation of variety to relieve the tedium.

She pulled out the large envelope that contained the week's insertions. That was her job on a Tuesday morning, to enter all the new inserts in the order book. It had taken some time to persuade Victor to stop 'showing her' how to do it every week and let her do it herself. Even now she had to fight with him to stop him doing it all on Monday nights after she had gone home, leaving her all Tuesday morning with nothing to do.

All the details then had to be transferred from the inserts book to a five-page form that went to Accounts. She had had to fight with him to stop him from keeping the forms locked up and dealing them out to her once a week with the date already written on the top. Relax her hold on her work even to go on holiday and Victor would be grabbing bits back from her to do himself, and she would be sitting idle, ready to scream, as he rushed about, tense and ferocious, complaining of being overworked and understaffed.

She took the forms out of their envelope and flicked through them. Victor had sorted them all into alphabetical order. She rammed them back into the envelope, put on her coat, and stalked out of the door.

It was 9.30.

The *Antiquarian's Weekly* was a venerable review with an unchanging format, ever predictable contents, and an increasingly elderly readership.

When Carrie had begun to work in the Classified Department she had been grateful for the loose atmosphere that allowed a radio and a toaster. But she had quickly come to learn that the actual work was done in an atmosphere of frustrated chaos. At first she had tried to help, but to help Victor was only to become as bitterly entangled as he was, while he first agreed with then subverted every idea she offered. And suggesting to Rawlings that all this confusion was not ideal was taken as a direct attack on his authority. Eventually she just pointedly ignored the pair of them. Rawlings called her sullen and uncooperative.

Yet for all this it was a woolly, flabby, smothering place. Any attempt to think through her situation lead straight from neatly labelled doors to confusing, winding, branching passages, so she was reduced to squabbling over petty complaints while the real problems were just pushed aside in dismay. She was used to hitting out, but here there was nothing to hit. Even Victor melted away at the moment of impact, to reappear wholly unfazed.

And day followed day with dismal regularity.

She wandered off down Oxford Street and looked in the shops, Victor and Rawlings rumbling about in her head. Then, when she managed to get them out of her thoughts, Swank took their place, which in some ways was even worse.

Swank had wanted to go out to the pub after Herbert had left. Carrie had been tired, much more than she should have been. She could find little joy these days in going out on a week night. She wanted to save her pleasures for the weekends, when they were not jammed tight between full days at work. Swank had gone off without her. She was somehow surprised that he still bothered to ask. When she left this fucking job they would have time to be together again, like before.

Swank had come back very late.

When she returned to the office, Carol was there. Five years before, when Carol had started at the *Weekly*, her children had still been young and she had wanted to see them safely off to school before she came to work, and get back home not too long after they did. So Mr Craig had agreed she would start at ten and finish at three, and even though it was no longer strictly necessary, the system had stuck.

'Hello,' said Carrie. She got on well with Carol.

'Look at this,' said Carol in a quiet voice, sounding annoyed. She showed Carrie the sheaf of work she had done the day before. On the bottom corner of each page Victor had written, quite unnecessarily, 'Okay V.S.', and stamped it with the *Antiquarian's Weekly* Classified Department stamp.

'What does he do that for?' Carrie wondered. Then, 'He's really been busy. Look at these.' And she laid out the alphabetically arranged insertions, finding it impossible not to giggle over them. 'What a fool.'

'And yet,' said Carol, 'when I came in here this morning I

heard him spending a good fifteen minutes telling Mr Rawlings how overworked he was.'

'Rawlings believes him. Rawlings takes it all in and thinks he really is poor hard-working Victor while we're lazy slobs who sit around doing nothing. Bastards.'

They had been through conversations like this a hundred times before on a hundred similar occasions. Carrie felt disgust creeping up on her again.

'Anyway,' she said. 'I don't care. I'm leaving soon.'

She put on the kettle to make some coffee. Rawlings came out of Victor's office.

'So,' he said, stopping short. 'You're back, are you?'

'Yup,' said Carrie.

'And where have you been, then?'

'Went for lunch.'

'You went for lunch, did you?'

'Yup.'

'You've had your lunch now, have you?'

'Yup.'

'Just so I know.' And he swaggered off to his own office, mercifully away down the passage.

'Arsehole,' she said.

She made her coffee. Carol was carefully unbuttoning her cardigan. Carrie stared, astonished and amused. Carol looked down, admiring the glitter sprinkled all over the bosom revealed by the low-cut dress.

'Do you like it? I just bought it yesterday. It'll come in useful when we go to the south of France again next year.' She took off her cardigan.

'Don't you think you ought to leave that on?' Carrie suggested.

'Nonsense.'

'It's too bad you weren't wearing that for your nude photos.'

'They weren't nude! They were semi-nude. Topless.' Carol grinned. 'I was thinking at our hen night last night, there were a couple of places I could have put this stuff.'

'Did you go? How was it?'

Half an hour later . . .

'And my John, he says, "How can you watch those men dress up like that, I think it's disgusting." And so I says, "Well what about those blue films you watch on the video, the things those women do to each other, arms and legs and tongues thrashing about all over the place, I think that's disgusting." '

Rawlings was suddenly back, in a raincoat. 'Are you ready, Victor?'

'Going for lunch together,' murmured Carol.

Victor came out with raincoat and umbrella. He switched off the lights of his office and locked the door.

'Been seeing a lot of each other lately,' Carol mused.

They went off together without noticing the two women.

'The things that go on, right under our noses.'

'What's he always want to lock his office door for?' Carrie demanded. 'What's he think he's got that we'd be interested in? It really gets to me, that does. He thinks he can poke through our stuff as much as he likes, but if he goes out for half an hour he locks his office up.'

'He's probably got pornography in there,' said Carol. 'Keeps it locked up in the safe.'

'That's all you think about after one of those hen nights.'

'My John says exactly the same.'

'Anyway,' Carrie said. 'If they've gone for lunch I don't have to do anything for the next hour.' She put the kettle on for more coffee.

'I'm off to lunch myself, now,' said Carol. 'Got some shopping to do.'

'Can I borrow your paper? I've read mine.'

It was twelve o'clock.

Wendy and Leonard were also just going for lunch. Wendy worked in Editorial, doing layout. Leonard worked in Accounts, a mere clerk. But Leonard could claim to be a poet. That is, he had had some poetry published in the university student magazine and in the smaller small magazines. Being a published poet impressed people, even though they never read any poetry. In fact, the less they knew about poetry, the more they were impressed.

They went off to lunch at the Red Lion. Leonard always found it too big, too full of grossly confident businessmen in their brashly jovial groups or alone with their willing and hungry office women. It was Wendy's favourite place.

Wendy asked, before they were hardly in the street, 'How's the writing going?'

Leonard said he was trying to get a volume of poetry together, which Wendy already knew, and that it was slow going. And it really was slow going. Accounting seeped into his brain like a smog, engrimed everything so that all he could see were the outlines, smothered him so effectively that only the occasional holiday could begin to blow things clear again. Privately, he doubted that the volume would ever be finished.

'On my holidays,' Wendy said, 'I went up into the hills and sat down and tried to write. But nothing would come.'

Leonard had been a brief but intriguing notion to Wendy. Much of the time he looked dull and shabby and demoralised. But she had persuaded him to let her see some of his work, and she was convinced it was good. She had two ideas of what successful poets were like – one was the bearded, pipe-smoking, Hampstead type, the other was the callous, passionate, Byronic hero. She was not sure which of these Leonard would metamorphose into once he was properly recognised, but either one meant an intellectual and social status that none of the other men she knew could provide. Of his proper recognition she was almost certain.

But she was also practical enough to believe she could do something with him in the meantime. Get him into nice clothes, shine his shoes, get him into something like advertising, creative but also lucrative. Just till they got established. He could write at weekends. She wrote herself, in a small way, and so together they would spend their lives in blissful creative communion.

Unfortunately Leonard did not play along with this romantic and appealing scenario. She dropped him whispers and smiles and glances and hints. She got him to take her to lunch. But Leonard was like an animal in a trap, convinced it was going to die there, with no hope of any way out. Wendy was just one more grey and lumpy object in the murk. If she had got him sacked so that the fog was suddenly swept away in a deluge of disruption, then he might have come to regard her with a retrospective affection. But she never thought of that.

Seated over their drinks, Wendy was telling him how enamoured she had become of Scotland. It had been *the* priority for her holidays. She had bought the Pelican *History of Scotland.* She wanted to write an historical novel about Scotland, about Scotland before the time of James VI. Mary Queen of Scots was her favourite historical figure. She meant to read Antonia Fraser's biography.

Leonard was tactless enough to say that he had never been greatly impressed by Mary Queen of Scots. He did not understand this sudden interest in Scotland. He mentioned John Fowles as a favourite modern novelist, and she beamed because she recognised the name. But she somehow felt they were not really communicating.

When Leonard sat studying her face so closely, as he was just now, it was not with the dawning emotion she had once hoped it would be. Rather he was thinking how much she looked like a photo in a fashion magazine. Clothes were his last line of defence. To work in a nine-to-five office job but not wear a suit or even a tie proved that he had not yet been wholly enslaved. But secretly he knew it was pointless. He was no different from the last decade's rebels he saw on the train going down to Surrey, their flowing hair attempting to belie their good clothes and their briefcases and their neatly knotted ties. Her superbly contrived appearance pushed her further away from him than ever.

So all in all, Leonard was proving something of a disappointment to Wendy, and she thought it was very convenient indeed that Willard had begun to make his desires clear.

Carrie got down to doing some work at about one. She put the radio on first. Rawlings and Victor arrived back at about 1.15. Rawlings scowled.

'Radio's a bit loud, isn't it?' he said.

'Sounds all right to me,' said Carrie.

'Well it doesn't sound all right to me.' He turned it down to just below audible.

'It always sounds too loud to you,' said Carrie.

He pushed his face right up in front of hers, a most offensive sight. 'Are you challenging me?'

'Suit yourself,' she shrugged.

She turned back to work, half acting haughty anger. And as she knew he would, he quickly back-pedalled trying to be reasonable.

'It's not me who objects,' he said. 'I don't mind. I don't mind at all. But what if Mr Craig were to come in and find the radio that loud? What then? Eh?'

His spinelessness disgusted her.

'I'll be back in a minute,' he called to Victor, and left.

'You don't mind the radio, do you, Victor?' she said, turning it back up.

'Oh no,' said Victor. 'No, not at all.'

The phone rang.

'Thought not,' she said, getting up to answer it. It was some old fool asking about prices.

'Victor,' she said, 'where are the new insertion rates?'

'What does he want?' Victor asked.

'He wants to know the prices for ads.'

'Tell him to write in for a price form.'

'Well if you give me the form I can tell him the prices over the phone.'

'No. He has to write in.'

She knew better than to bother arguing. She explained to the man that he had to write in for a form. He asked if they could send him one, and she began to take down his address.

'No,' said Victor, catching her hand. 'He has to write in enclosing the proper return postage and we'll send it out to him. That's the point of having the forms at all. If he doesn't want to do that the prices are in the magazine.'

'That's stupid, Victor,' she said. 'And he says he doesn't have the magazine with him.'

'That's how it's done.'

'But it's not. We just tell them over the phone.'

'What's this then?' Rawlings demanded, eyeing her from the door.

She explained to the man what he had to do then hung up in the middle of his protests, hoping he would change his mind and forget the whole thing.

'What's this then?' Rawlings said again.

'What's what then?' she retorted.

Rawlings had no idea what it was, except that Carrie was in the middle of it. He cast about for something more definite that she was responsible for.

'That radio's up again, isn't it?'

'Is it?' she said. 'I hadn't noticed.'

'Suppose someone comes on the phone,' Rawlings said, beginning to raise his voice. 'How are you going to hear them with the radio like that?'

'Someone just was on the phone. I could hear him perfectly.'

The thing about Rawlings was you could not even have a decent fight with him. Carol came back just as he slunk off to his office.

'Hello,' she said. 'Have I missed something?'

'You're kidding,' said Carrie.

Blessedly, the twosome spent the afternoon, as they often did, hidden away in Rawlings's office, for which Carrie was marginally grateful. But she still sighed wearily long before the afternoon was ended, and complained of being fed up.

'Cheer up,' said Carol. 'It's Christmas soon.'

'I don't know if I'm coming back after Christmas.'

She glanced over at Carol and saw how perturbed she looked. Carol complained about having to come in to work on a regular cycle; a few days of accepting it, a few days of threatening to get pregnant and quit. Yet now she looked as if one of her children was seriously proposing to do something both odd and dangerous.

'It's not too bad,' she said. 'And with all this unemployment you might never get another job.'

'I don't want another job. I'd rather be on the dole. People say the dole's boring, but it's not a tenth as boring as this. What if I had to do this for the next ten years, what sort of zombie do you think I'd be by the end of it?'

'Other people manage.'

'Well I'm not like other people.'

When pressed as to why she stayed on if she did not want to, Carol always pointed out that only thus could they afford the double glazing, the new kitchen, the video recorder, or the boat.

She said, 'Maybe they'd let you work part time instead.'

'I asked about that,' said Carrie. 'I asked Rawlings. I told him I could get all my work done in three days instead of five and so couldn't I have the other two days off. Victor was there. Rawlings says to him, "I thought you said we were up to our necks in it?" and Victor says, "We are." And that was that.'

'They're a stupid pair, aren't they,' Carol said, climbing hastily back on to safer ground.

'Thing is, Rawlings has been going around saying we need a third person working with us to take the load off Victor. So he's not going to agree to me being here only half the week.'

At work the next day there was to be a party in the lunch hour. It was for Debbie, a girl in Circulation who a week and a half before, had left. She had given in her proper notice, there had been a going-away party for her on her last day, and she had said all her final goodbyes. And then, just a week later, she had returned, asking in a small voice if she could have her old job back. So now there was to be a coming-back party. Although this time Debbie had to pay for the drinks.

All of them grumbled about their work at one time or another. They complained in the same way they complained about the weather or the buses. None of them had any real idea of doing anything about it.

'I've been here over eight months already,' Carrie said. 'The longer I stay the more I'll accept it and the harder it will be to quit.'

'Well I don't know,' said Carol. 'You don't want to give up a good job at a time like this.'

When Carrie got home the empty flat was dark and cold and smelling of damp. She put on the light, put on the heat, but remained in her coat, pacing about, trying to pin down her thoughts.

Assimilation is something that just happens to people. It takes great amounts of energy to refuse it. Carrie identified herself with a bristling mass of assertions and assumptions just as surely as any pert secretary or care-worn housewife. But her choice was idiosyncratic. Assimilation into the *Antiquarian's Weekly* was something she would resist with her last breath, and the inescapable daily friction of her battle was beginning to tear away at just those things she thought most essential to herself. Answering back, fighting back, being her own boss.

Carol had the right idea about work. Carol took the guise of a coarse and cheerful chameleon and survived intact. Carrie was a prickly urchin, wearing herself away just in keeping at bay the final acceptance.

She had had a dream a few nights ago of a cat, meowing at her in frustration, trying to communicate something of importance in a language she could not understand. Or had forgotten.

She did not see why she could not just survive at this in the same way she had always survived at anything else. It seemed as if there was something inside her that she was searching for but not finding, some true north.

The thing that causes so much trouble with casual telepathy is that after a while you no longer know if it is you thinking about her or her thinking about you, and it becomes so chaotic and disturbed you have to dump the whole thing just to give your brain a rest. Circulation, Victor, Rawlings, they seeped into her soul like a bad smell into wool.

Swank arrived home.

'This place stinks,' he said, barely looking at her. 'Why don't you open a fucking window.'

'It's the damp,' she said. 'It makes it smell all musty.'

How was it Swank never seemed to worry or become miserable? Swank got depressed, he got violent, he cheered up again the next morning. Swank never seemed to sense something was wrong. Swank was not becoming vulnerable in the way that she suddenly seemed to be. How fortunate to be Swank and to always have a tough, confident face to turn to the world.

She followed him into the kitchen, where he was unwrapping a couple of pies and sticking them in the oven.

'Been out?' she asked, tentatively.

'Been to see a band,' he said.

Both pies would be for him. She glanced around the shelves but could find no desire for anything except the cereal she had not bothered with in the morning.

'Anyone we know?' she rinsed clean a bowl.

'Yeh. Well, I dunno if you know them. Pete Reed and them? I'm going to be their manager.'

'No, I don't know them.' Rice Krispies. Crackle crackle. Like static.

'You might know them if you got out of the house a bit more.'

She said nothing.

'Anyway, we was hoping you could do us a poster. Something using the British Movement symbol.'

'Oh God, Swank, what are you getting involved in all that for?'

He looked annoyed. 'They're entitled to their own opinions, aren't they?' It's my affair, his voice said. You needn't get involved if you don't feel like it.

'Swank, no one but a few skins are going to support them. They won't get on the radio. The music papers won't write about them. There'll be aggro at all their gigs. All you're doing is asking to get your head kicked in.'

'Rubbish,' said Swank. He opened a bottle of Guinness.

'Anyway,' he went on, 'you were saying yourself how many fucking blacks there are around here. So don't go getting all holy. I can see through that.'

'I'm not getting all holy.'

'Anyway,' he said, 'they're good, and I'm going to manage them. Just wait till you hear them before you judge them, all right?'

'All right. I just didn't know you'd become such a businessman.'

'Huh! Look who's talking – Secretary of the Year.'

'Come on, Swank. You always hated all that. You hated anything to do with the business end of things. You know you did.'

Warning signals were triggering in her stomach, telling her to pull back before she started a serious row. If Swank wanted to manage a band, good for him. What was she getting so upset about?

'Your pies will be ready,' she mumbled.

'You've become a right misery since you've been working at that place,' said Swank. He balanced the pies one on top of another and took them through to the other room to eat them.

She closed the oven door and put her bowl in the sink. She felt thirsty, but could not decide what to drink. She made a cup of tea.

'Swank,' she said, joining him. 'I want to leave work.'

'So leave,' he said.

'But what about the money?'

'We always survived before.'

Where had all the extra money gone? This place cost a bit more because it was two rooms and a kitchen, but not all that much. It was a lot to go through just to have a few more pounds to fritter away.

'You think I should?'

'Why not?'

'Won't you need money for your band?'

'Look, if you want to quit then quit. You've got to take control of your life, Carrie. You can't just dither about for ever.'

Poor Swank. He had not thought much of the idea right from the start. She must have been making his life miserable with all her moping about.

'Actually though,' he said. 'Maybe you should hold on to it. It does make you independent, and you never know when you might need that. I mean, this place isn't much, but it could be a bit more than you could manage just by yourself on the dole.'

It took a moment for the implications of this to get through to her.

'What do you mean?' Worried.

'I'm just saying, you never know what could happen. It could be useful having that money coming in some day. You might need it.'

'Well I did it for you as well so we could have more things.' She could feel unaccustomed tears welling up, just below the surface.

'Oh Christ,' said Swank. He was getting up, putting his jacket back on.

'All right, I will leave. Then I can come and see your band. We'll have time to do things again, like before.'

He was standing at the open door, looking back at her.

'You never do fuck all anyway,' he said, and left.

Wendy, that evening, was attending an informal dinner gathering at the elegant and comfortable Sussex home of Mr Heron. Mr Heron was the owner of the *Antiquarian's Weekly*, although his actual income was derived from other sources. Also present were his wife, Grace, Mr Craig, the managing director of the

Antiquarian's Weekly, with his wife, and Willard Heron, Mr Heron's only son.

Mr Heron was a shy man who had had to learn to hide his shyness and had done so with such effect that the possession of money was something that he no longer even thought about. Willard had inherited the shyness, but had had no cause to develop any further.

'. . . in Scotland, last summer,' Mr Heron was saying. He and his son still wore tartans on formal occasions.

Grace Heron gave a warm polite laugh. 'I don't think Wendy has the first idea what we're talking about,' she said.

'Oh, I do. I love Scotland. My parents came from Northumberland, which is about as close as you can get.'

'Yes, Willard was saying.'

'I think Scotland has retained such a strong identity,' said Wendy. 'England's identity has been diffused and diluted, what with the New Commonwealth and all those blacks claiming to be British, and the stupidities of the Left. While Scotland is still Scotland.'

'Mind you,' said Mr Heron. 'There are those who would like to ruin Scotland the same way they've ruined England.'

'It never ends, does it,' said Mr Craig. 'Why, up in Guildford . . .'

During the course of the meal someone mentioned Leonard, causing some quiet laughter, with which Wendy joined as easily as anyone else.

Willard and Wendy could not share a bed. She would have known better than to do so, anyway. They kissed at the top of the stairs. His shyness would become sensitivity with the proper handling, and his intelligence was good, and so were his teeth. And she knew he was someone she could implicitly trust. He was thirty-two but she was twenty-five. They kissed again and said goodnight, she lingering at her door until he had disappeared behind his.

He was, without a doubt, a much better bet.

The party the next day was being held in Circulation, this being considered more homely and familiar than a pub, and they brought in cakes and pizza to go with the booze. Carol and

Carrie were invited, of course, but Rawlings and Victor were not. The girls in Circulation were a ragamuffin mob at the best of times, and now the whole floor rang with their squeals and excited laughter long before lunchtime began.

Carrie was not really looking forward to it. Although she knew it would be all right once she got going. She had gone to bed alone very early last night, and had woken up alone very early that morning. She certainly was not in a partying mood. Maybe it would cheer her up.

Circulation had everything well under way by the time they arrived, but there seemed to be an exchange of looks when they saw Carrie that they did not understand. It was gone in an instant, she could almost believe she had imagined it. A girl pressed a drink into her hand and began talking to her at inordinate length.

All Carrie's conversation abandoned her, so she just grinned inanely and answered as best she could. Two people standing close by seemed to be laughing at her. She started to feel uncomfortable.

When the girl drifted away she made for the nearest familiar face, which happened to be Wendy, and they exchanged a few words about their plans for Christmas. Wendy was known all over the building and was a popular favourite. She at least was acting normally.

Carrie said she was thinking of going back up to Yorkshire for Christmas, although she had had no such plans until a second ago. Wendy said she could well be going to Scotland. Then Anne came up to speak to Wendy, and Carrie drifted away.

People had formed into two groups. None of the people she knew seemed to be there. She tried to squeeze between the two circles, and spilt wine on herself and possibly on someone else, she did not dare turn back to look. She began to feel self-conscious and went to stand by the window, looking out over the street. But standing there alone made her feel all the more uneasy and out of place, so she turned back to the party.

Where was Carol? And the girls from Circulation? Where, even, was Debbie, the cause of the whole party? It was so dull in the room that she could not see the faces properly, but she was sure there was no one here she knew. She felt a vague surprise that there should be so many people working here that she had never met.

She finally spotted Carol talking to someone, but she did not like to go over and interrupt. Carol's face was in the centre of a circle of brightness, the last brightness visible, and as Carrie turned her thoughts from her the circle shrank away to nothing and the whole room, from the waist up, was enshrouded in dusk. She could make out the features of not one person, not one. Her ears buzzed lightly. She could hear nothing else.

She walked to a table to put down her glass, feeling desolate and alone, conspicuous and ungainly, standing there like a fool, talking to no one, in a room full of strangers.

She finally spied a familiar figure, Victor's tall back, his head bowed self-consciously, standing on the edge of one of the groups, pretending he was part of it all, ignored.

'Well I'm not going to do that,' she muttered, and headed for the door. No one noticed her, and she prayed no one would stop her so that she would not have to make a fool of herself.

She went and hid in the toilets for five minutes.

It had all happened horribly fast.

Carrie arrived home early in the afternoon, and disturbed Swank packing a suitcase in the bedroom.

'Oh, hello,' he said, as if nothing unusual was happening.

'What's going on?' she said, and sat down on the bed. All of his clothes were gone. Through the door she could see the back of the sofa where he had left a box of records tied up with a piece of string and his guitar. She had seen them as she came in. They made the place look insecure.

'Swank?'

Swank finally stood still and looked at her.

'I just thought I'd go and stay with a friend for a while, sort of a change. You know how stale we've been getting. I thought we'd benefit from a change. You've been looking like you could use some time to yourself.'

He was fastening the suitcase. Her head felt numb.

'Who?'

'No one, really. Well, you know Sandra, don't you?'

Sandra? Only vaguely.

'Sandra?'

'Yeh, she's a nice kid. We've been seeing a lot of each other.'

He picked up his case. He seemed to be fearing some sort of explosion, but she sat too stunned for that.

'Anyway, I know where to find you, so I'll be in touch, all right?'

She sat and watched him carry suitcase and records out of the flat, heard a car door slam in the lane, saw him come back for the guitar and another smaller bag she had not noticed.

'I think that's the lot. Okay?'

She said nothing.

He came and stood in the doorway.

'Okay?'

She nodded.

He looked uncertain.

'Yeh, well. Okay. See you.'

The door shut behind him. She heard him get into the car. She heard them drive off. Then she heard nothing. Just the sounds of a big empty flat. Where nothing ever moved. And no one ever said anything. Like a grainy photograph with a dusty taste.

She lay down on the bed, and then, because she was cold, she kicked off her shoes and got beneath the blankets, still in her coat and make-up. And after a while the room got darker as the sun went down. And after a while she fell asleep.

Wendy got married two months later and went to live in a big house in Edinburgh, from where she sent out into the world a steady stream of very successful historical romances.

ALISON

Alison was sitting in a middle-aged night spot in south London on a Friday night, talking to Terry Watkins from Brighton. Terry was a promoter who had already got her a lot of new work along the coast and was now trying to move in on London as well. He had a small moustache, he wore a tired suit, and his face shone.

He wanted her to be more modern.

Alison was ragging him.

'What do you want me to do, Terry? I could always take off my clothes and roll about on splinters of glass and call it Art. That would be really modern, that would. Avant-garde, even. The front line. Never been done before. Well, not often, anyway. And never on BBC 1.'

Her scented breath, her artistic make-up, and her quicker wit always put Terry at a disadvantage.

'That's not what I meant . . .'

'You want me to have a more disco feel. Quicker rhythms, flashing lights, a backing chorus.'

'Right.' He smiled now.

'I don't like disco.'

His face dropped.

'Terry, either you're right on top of these styles, doing them the moment they appear, solely because you love them, or else you don't bother. You don't jump on a bandwagon five years after it's started. The only thing that will get you is looking stupid and washed up.'

'Look,' said Terry, 'all I know is this. Some of the clubs you like to sing, their managers have told me they'd like you better if your sound was more modern.'

'I like what I sing.'

'All I'm saying is: you see you, I see your image. Your image is ten or fifteen years older than you are. Your image is rapidly becoming very early-morning Radio Two. That's not good for you and it's not good for me. I'm just saying you've got to be a little more modern.'

Irritation looked all the more petulant on such a carefully constructed face.

'What is modern, Terry? Disco is old fashioned now. The modern thing is synthesisers and all that crap. I've heard those bands, and all I hear are the same old pop songs dressed up in funny new clothes. Nothing new. Just fashion. Forget it, Terry. There's no such thing. I sing what I want to sing.'

He shrugged patiently. He told her they'd discuss it all with Bree. See what could be done with her act without adding anything she didn't like. Which meant Bree was in on this, too.

'Well you'll have to wait a while. I'm on holiday starting tomorrow.'

He flashed the PR smile. 'Anywhere interesting?'

'Thirsk. North Yorkshire.'

'Thirsk? What the hell is there to do in Thirsk?'

She sat back and took a good long look at this Terry Watkins, and realised how much she was coming to dislike him and what he represented. She picked up her bag and stood up.

'I used to live there,' she said. She turned to leave without bothering to nod goodbye. He was startled by her abruptness, but was unable to take it personally.

'Send me a postcard,' he called after her.

Back at her flat Alison peeled off her glittering clothes and wiped off her make-up. She sat silent in an armchair, looking at nothing.

She resented Bree sending her off to entertain Terry the night before her holidays. She wanted to forget all that for a bit. Now what he had said would nag at her, unless she was able to bury it somewhere until she came back.

Early-morning Radio Two.

The phone startled her, and she sat frozen until it stopped. Then she took it off the hook, made some coffee, and put on an old Sandie Shaw record.

For the Eurovision Song Contest in 1967 Sandie Shaw had done five weekly appearances on the Rolf Harris show. Alison had been . . . eight? Sandie Shaw had worn mini-skirts and looked very glamorous. She and Rolf Harris always had a bit of a laugh between them.

Every week she sang one of the five songs that were being considered as Britain's entry, and viewers were supposed to write in voting for their favourite. One week she began the song descending a long flight of stairs as the intro music played, starting the song near the bottom. She sang perhaps a verse and a half, then she was suddenly quiet and said, 'Could you stop the music, please?'

Everyone in Britain looked at her blankly.

'Could you stop the music, please?'

The music tugged itself to a halt.

Silence.

A small voice.

'I think I came in at the wrong time. Could we start over again?'

The music started over again. Walking down the stairs had given her something to do while the intro played. Now she had to stand nervously at the bottom, trying to look nonchalant.

She reached the right moment and began to sing again. It is doubtful that one in fifty could have noticed the difference. Afterwards it was all smiles, and Rolf Harris said something like, 'Were you scared?' and Sandie Shaw said, 'My heart was just thumping,' and everyone laughed.

Eight-year-old Alison used to daydream about standing at the bottom of those stairs, before the audience and the TV cameras and the eyes of the world and all her friends, saying, magnificently and painfully, 'Could you stop the music, please?'

Still, of course . . .

Sandie Shaw would not have hits with that sort of material today. She did not really have constant successes back in 1967.

And Alison had yet to have one record reach number 98.

She switched off the album halfway through the last song on side one, and ran a bath.

Then, scrubbed and dried and sleepy, she went to bed.

The train left King's Cross at 8 a.m. She had a newspaper and a magazine, a carton of orange juice and a bag of peanuts-and-raisins to help her through the journey. It was cloudy and it would probably rain, but she had forgotten to bring her light jacket in case it turned out sunny and warm.

She read a little and she dozed a little and she looked out of the window. As they drew into Doncaster her thoughts were sent back to the days when she used to go down there with the old gang, sometimes, on weekend nights.

That had been in the days when she went slumming, looking for novelty and guts. Swank had been calling himself a club poet, talking his way on to gigs to do his bit between sets. No one ever paid any attention to him. People often assumed he was just one of the audience suddenly seized with drunken inspiration, and sometimes they followed suit and got up to do their own impromptu performances. Once, two girls got a second microphone switched on and started singing Twist and Shout in the middle of one of his poems. And once, after he had finished, a Czech expatriate dissident, grey hair and life-lined face, got up with an acoustic guitar and sang a song about freedom in (presumably) Czechoslovakian.

Swank had short hair even then, prison style, when everyone else still had shoulder-length locks and flares. Carrie was already on the streets, done up like Bet Lynch. She used to follow Swank around the clubs. It was Carrie that Alison got to know first – she always felt a little wary of Swank – and though they later lost touch they continued to remember each other.

One night, having gone down by bus, Swank, typical Swank, decided he would steal a car to get them back home. And soon they were roaring up the motorway and some of the girls were saying, 'Slow down, we don't want the police to stop us in a stolen car.' And Swank was saying, 'What the fuck,' and the boys thought it was great and that if they were going to be caught with a stolen car they might as well have some fun first.

They had pulled in at a lay-by and two of the boys had been on the roof and they had made a dent. And then the aerial got broken off. And then – what was his name? Rob? – Rob wanted to ride on the roof, and he had lain down flat with his hands coming in at the top of the door windows, gripping on for life, while Swank drove at a steady 30 m.p.h., going up to 40 sometimes to give Rob a scare, but still taking it easy on the corners. And they could hear Rob singing at the top of his voice, and any minute they expected his hands to slip from sight and see him spread out on the road behind them.

Then Rob got back into the car, and it was as well he did, for they crashed into a parked car just inside the city. They got out a little shaken but unhurt. They had hit the car with just their front corner, but everything was all bent in and the light was smashed and they decided they had better clear off.

So they walked back through the streets of nice houses, with their hedges and their brick walls and their tall trees. And the boys were giving each other boosts up to see what was over the top of each wall, and one of the gardens had a swimming pool in it. There were no lights on in the house, and so it was over the fence and the boys were stripped and naked and into the pool. They called to the girls, but only Carrie was willing. She tugged off her clothes and was in with them while the other two watched from the side.

Then they got tired of that pool and went looking for another one, three naked boys and one naked girl (fighting off teasing hands on all sides) and two fully clothed girls, parading down respectable suburban avenues, looking for a place to swim. Alison courageously pulled off blouse and bra, but then a police car drifted by and they had to run.

They thought better of more nude frolicking after that, and they got dressed and eventually split up and went home.

How long since she had seen any of them?

Going back to the place you have lived in for the first twelve years of your life, and then not seen even once for the second twelve years of your life, was like watching a once-loved, almost-forgotten film. Although you knew the general outline well enough, most of the details had been lost until you saw them again. Then they were suddenly so familiar it was as if you had still been walking past them every day just as recently as yesterday.

There were differences. The very station platform had been altered. Fenced off through-lines in the middle, stopping local lines on the outside. But there, still, was the foot bridge, and the large white guest house by the station car park, and on the long walk into town there were the same houses, still evoking the funny, too-new feel they had always had for her, and there was every green railing, turnstile and noticeboard of the race-track. And always could be seen the hills, brown and green and pale in the distance. It was like hypnotism, where your mind can throw up all sorts of pointless details that you could have no reason at all for remembering. She seemed to recognise almost each step of her way, as if she had just designed it herself.

Town end, and the short cut through Castle Garth, a field where there had once been a castle. You went that way to get to the doctor's and this way to get to the town centre. There was the building with the high railings over which Andrew from school had lost his plastic man on a parachute. Her conscious memory had forgotten that the field was so hummocky. Her subconscious memory seemed to recognise every curve.

Through the little wooden gate into the shaded alley. The Club Selecta now called itself the Pandora. It had a brand new wooden door, but was otherwise just as haughtily inconspicuous as ever. There was another door farther down, with a couple of worn-down steps. When she was still very young and had come across the strange and intriguing notion that something as insubstantial as footsteps could wear away something as hard and solid as stone, these very steps had provided her with much fascinated musing while her mother was in the butcher's on the corner.

And there was the same butcher's. And you turned this way, around the corner, and there, there, was the familiar, ordinary, disorganised, enchanting marketplace with its Saturday stalls and its cobbles and its tall town clock, just as she remembered it. It was like when you wake up suddenly from a strange dream to find your own bedroom with all the normal colours and sounds and feelings of morning. Or it was like those dreams where you are young again, twelve years old, going precisely and mundanely from A to B with never a thought for how nostalgia and distance could make too-familiar A and too-trivial B so magical and wonderful. When you had dreams like that you tried to hold on to them and turn them into daydreams, and cursed having to get up and be prosaic and mundane all over again, even if it was as a night-club singer in far-away, fabulous London.

She looked at the people. She did not even dare to hope for a familiar face. What does someone look like you last saw when you were twelve? Altered beyond all recognition. The people looked different from London people. The boys looked more youthful than their apparent age, and their quaint hairstyles and somehow more mellow clothes gave them a rather soft look. The women looked rounded, but full of health and good humour rather than full of fat. Their faces seemed more open, somehow more sincere. The familiar Yorkshire accents made their voices seem kindlier, just as all London voices had once sounded sophisticated. The people behind the shop counters always smiled at you.

All was familiar, all was welcome, all seemed welcoming. The fish and chip shop where she bought her lunch, the little pub which she had often passed but had never till today been inside. The Golden Fleece hotel, imposing once, with the air of a strict and elderly aunt, where she had gone every Thursday for her ballet lessons. The huge old mill by the river had been torn down; there could not possibly be room on such a tiny space of ground for so immense a building. The Green, neglected and shabby when she had lived there, was spruce and peaceful and cared for at last. Beyond it was the river again, the Beck, and beside the river a little path with a rickety white fence, not now so white but much more rickety. The river flowed under the bridge and past the infants' school and out into the Flats Fields.

This little infants' school had been first, but it was the junior school that made more sense to her in her memory, as if by then she had finally developed a mind of her own instead of being just a malleable receptacle for essential skills. So at the junior school she ignored the 'No Trespassing' signs at the gates and went right up to look in the windows of her old classrooms.

They looked unchanged. Just shabbier. The very same desks, she was certain, clean and new in the late sixties, worn, scratched and graffitied in the early eighties. Perhaps with the very same texts inside, just as worn and shabby. They were even arranged in the same order except that, curiously, in each room the teachers' desks were in the wrong place. They looked improbably small and quaint. It was all strange and remarkable. The memories made her feel warm.

The junior school had been fifteen minutes' walk each morning, but the comprehensive was even farther, right up at the end of Topcliffe Road, almost on the very edge of town. But then they had moved to the new estate in Saxty Way, and school had been almost just across the street. It was a creation of the sixties, big and modern, with long corridors and a bewildering layout that had the First Formers wandering about lost for days.

She walked across the front playground. Once, when she had forgotten her gym clothes for the third successive time she had been sent out here to pick up litter. She had dawdled her way to the front door, had stopped to read the noticeboard, and had been jumped on by some busybody woman teacher who demanded to know what she thought she was doing. She had explained, in a bored sort of voice, naïvely certain the teacher would see the stupidity of the punishment. But the teacher had said, 'If you have been told to pick up litter then you had better go and do so.' It had been very humiliating.

She looked in the windows of the science rooms, but could not see much because of the blinds. They used to be marched along to this biology room every Tuesday afternoon, and Janice, swinging her arms absent-mindedly in the crowded corridor, had once caught some kid behind her in the balls, a cause for much giggling.

It was on this playground and the large field behind the school that she and the boys she had known for years began to see each other in new ways. She had only been here a year. Suppose she had stayed? Would she have ended up marrying one of them? And then what?

She wandered around the edge of the large south wing, past the room where they had art and the class Christmas party, and past the room where the girls had been taught to cook while the boys went off for woodwork. It had to be said that cooking was probably more useful, in the general daily run of things, than woodwork. Unless, of course, you could expect to have a wife to do it for you.

There were buildings she did not really remember here, on the other side of the south wing. Surely this land had once been just an open field, stretching from here to the road. She had sat in class on boring afternoons and watched the wind make waves in the tall grass or crops or whatever grew there. She could not be sure which was her old window now. Somewhere in the middle. They all looked the same. One room had walls covered in maps and charts. A pile of exercise books on the window-ledge caught her eye. 'Karen', said the top one, confidently, as if there could only possibly be one Karen in the world. '3C, Mr Jenkins, History.' She did not remember a Mr Jenkins. She looked in the window of the music room. The piano, the same piano, was in the same place, although there was no way of knowing who might teach music from behind it now.

She went to visit their old next-door neighbour in Saxty Way, but no one was home.

Down the lane to the Flats Fields, with their eternal trees and their eternal rises and hollows and their eternal cows. Past the swimming baths that had not been built when she lived there. Through one of the little alleys that she remembered almost by instinct. And back into the marketplace.

There was nothing much left to do. Ten years before she had written her last letter to old friends in this town. She could not find their names in the phone book. Perhaps they weren't on the phone. She walked past the door of 36 Long Street without asking if Janet still lived there. Janet undoubtedly did not.

A female voice behind her said, 'I've never seen her around Thirsk before.' She did not look back to see if it was really herself that was being referred to. She began to feel lonely and conspicuous.

She had been up since dawn. She had been walking about here since 10.30 a.m. It was time to go home, put her feet up, and watch TV. Yet in this town that seemed to her more familiar than her own flat in Hammersmith there was no proper home for her to go to. It felt very odd.

And there was something else missing, too. A clue. Some

clue from her past that would tell her just what was going on in her present and where she should look for her future. She expected to come across it in the curve of some familiar street, or in the eyes of some quiet, brooding house, or by a shifting together of the pieces so that they would suddenly click into place and all make sense. But there was no shifting, no revelation. No sense.

One clue. A group of teenage girls, sixteen or seventeen years old, walking up Topcliffe Road. In her mind, Thirsk and her twelve-year-old self always went together. She could not imagine herself here at any intermediate stage between then and now. Even now she was trying to see it all again through the eyes of then. The girls reminded her that her twelve-year-old self had to grow up. It did not really seem to be the clue she was looking for.

She walked up Kirkgate to the church. She had been sent here every Sunday as a child. Big, old. In winter, yellow-lit and friendly, in summer, cool and shaded. They had come here once on a class outing when she was about ten, and they were eagerly signing their names in the visitors' book when the teacher and the vicar came hurrying up to scold them and erase their signatures. Now, with a mischievous smile playing across her lips and a sense of an injustice finally righted, she signed her name again. There was no rush of angry authority, but she heard the big door open and close and a dark, robed figure came to stand beside her, demanding an explanation.

'London, eh?'

She felt embarrassed at being caught.

'Staying with us long?'

'Just a few days.'

He was young, with a light beard. The curate, she thought.

She looked around the church.

'I don't really believe in all this,' she said. 'But I like churches. They're so old and silent. They're full of something you can't see.'

'If you can't see it, how do you know it's there?' he said, asking the obvious.

She shrugged. 'I can understand the basic idea. I just have trouble squaring that with what goes on in the world. Same as a lot of other people.'

'Reminds me of my sermon last week,' he said. Did curates give sermons? Maybe it was the vicar after all.

'There is a crack in the tiles around my bath,' he went on. 'And the other day a little spider found its way out on to the ledge and then plummeted straight over the side into the bath. The bath was empty, fortunately, but the sides were too steep and smooth for him to climb back up. He was trapped, and he knew he was trapped, and he kept trying to scramble up at one place after another. I didn't want to pick him up with my fingers in case I injured him, so I put a small piece of paper in front of him, expecting him to crawl on to it. Well, he may have been desperate, but he wasn't stupid. Half-a-dozen times I put the paper down in front of him, and each time he was having none of it. Finally I had to knock his legs from under him and carry him rolled up in a little ball and dump him on the edge of the bath. Except he was now upside down, helplessly waving his legs in the air, and I had to nudge him again with the paper to get him the right way up.

'And once he was up he turned round and walked right back towards the drop. I banged against the bath to scare him away. He stopped, then moved closer again. I banged again. Finally he went off in the other direction and found the putty around the tiles. This seemed to be more like it, something he recognised, and he began to crawl along that. He crawled a good three feet in the wrong direction, and even if he'd been going in the right direction he was too low down and would have missed the crack anyway. Finally he decided he was going the wrong way and turned around to crawl a foot or so in the other direction. Then he turned round again, then again, six inches this way, a foot that, completely lost.

'So finally I put the piece of paper down in front of him again. He hesitated a moment, then stepped on to the very edge, no further than that, and waited. I picked up the paper and deposited him, again rolled up in a tight little ball, almost right inside his crack in the tiles. He unrolled himself, walked in the wrong direction for two seconds, and then realised where he was, turned, and disappeared back into the wall. Safe at last.'

He stopped.

'So?' said Alison.

'So . . .'

'So we're all spiders and God helps us out when we're in trouble, but sometimes He just squashes us and washes us down the plughole. Is that it?'

'Ah, sort of, although I'm not sure about the last part. But there's more to it than that. Think of that spider, young and inexperienced probably, but clever and adventurous as well or he would never have wandered from the safety behind the tiles. He was lost, scared, confused, desperate. Think of the courage it took to step on to that piece of paper which before he had been so anxious to avoid. Think of the immense faith it took to trust his very life to a force that seemed to offer help but one he could not even begin to understand. Just think of that.'

Alison thought.

'I think you're crazy,' she laughed.

He did not take offence. He laughed with her.

'You know very well what I mean,' he said. 'And you know I'm right.'

She shook her head.

'It's all right for you,' she said. 'But it's different if you can't get off the dole, or you can't get out of your boring self-destructive job, or you can't get a decent place to live in.' Or you can't get a record in the Top 40.

'No,' he said. 'It's not different.'

But she wasn't so sure. She said goodbye and left.

It was getting on for five o'clock. It could soon start to rain. She walked to the bed and breakfast where she had booked a room and ate a supper of bananas and oranges while she read the paper. She would not go to the Pandora Club as she had contemplated doing. It would probably be full of Heavy Metal rustics, naïve small-town youths who would try to chat her up, and jealous small-town girls who would say vicious things to her in the toilets. But if not that, then what? It was too early to go to bed. Yet her legs ached, so she kicked off some of her clothes and lay down on the quilt a while to rest. She quickly fell asleep.

The road from Thirsk to Sutton Bank, where the land rises sharply to become the western edge of the Yorkshire Moors, is simple and utilitarian. It passes through only one village, a mere string of houses, and exists for the sole purpose of getting traffic from point to point. And so, like the others of its kind, it is completely lacking in footpaths and, most of the way, even in the flat grass verges that could be used instead of footpaths. You can walk on the side facing the oncoming traffic and step almost into the middle of the hedge every time a car goes by, but that will not save you from being buzzed within an inch of your life by cars coming up behind you that just have to overtake each other right there and then. The scenery, however, can be quite pleasant.

On the other hand, if you know the area from when you were young, and if you have a map in case your memory is not quite good enough, you can take the road that branches off to the left as you leave Thirsk, walk through country that ascends gently, yet with quiet drama up into the hills, amid scenery that can be much more than simply pleasant, and have an almost car-free time of it into the bargain.

So when Alison walked up the hill and around the corner into Felixkirk, under a sky that was blue and warm, past a pub that was firmly closed, and in her too-warm coat in case it rained, she did not feel at all like someone who had just walked three miles and had who knows how many more to go. She felt like someone who was leaving all her cares behind her and had nothing to do for the day but concentrate on the present and on not getting lost.

She sat on a small hill, round and high for its diameter, and ate an orange as a reward for getting this far. It was a pretty enough village. A more cynical eye might have called it unexceptional, although the architecture of its church seemed unusual, and the tree-shrouded mount rising up behind it gave it a slight air of mystery; and a more aesthetic eye might have found it unadorned, although the road bent to the left then wound about the churchyard, to give the impression that the village was not just another string of houses.

She wished she lived somewhere like this, in one of these plain, solid houses, with the hill behind and the vale in front. Going to church on Sundays, buying eggs and cheese straight from the farms. She would need a car, of course, as the buses were bound to be infrequent. How nice it would be to have not a car but a horse, and go riding about the country free of both mechanical worries and aching feet. Although you would need a car as well, for business trips. Not that she could afford a car and a horse. Not that she could really afford a car *or* a horse. Not that she could afford to live here at all. Unless she gave up singing and found a job in Thirsk, or York, or unless she just came up here whenever she had the opportunity. In which case she would have to maintain a flat in London and a house here and pay for all those train fares as well. It couldn't be done.

She threw her orange peel into the long grass and stood to brush the thoughts away before they could darken her mood. She looked at the map. This hill was a 'motte'. Some shaggy, ancient Briton warrior king had been buried here. Or was it some slightly less shaggy Saxon warrior king? Or was it not a gravesite at all but the remnants of a castle that once stood here, perhaps a simple mound with a barricade of whole tree trunks halfway up its height. Or had the castle actually been across the road, where the writing on the map was, or was it just that there was not room on the map to write 'motte' on this side of the road? And what exactly was a motte anyway?

She walked around the churchyard, looking for old graves with ancient dates, but she did not go inside because there was a service on and she would look foolish arriving in the middle. She had been to church exactly twice since she was thirteen and her parents considered her old enough to leave it to her own conscience. Perhaps if you went to an old old church in a setting like this on a morning like this, with the real world all around you and the concrete, busy human world far away, perhaps then it all became clear and the whole thing meant something. But it probably did not. She walked as far as the end of the village, retraced her steps, and took the side road off towards Thirlby.

She knew well why it attracted her, this ancient land with its dusty, stony roads and its rough, quiet fields and its wide, gently tumbling scenery. And she knew why the seduction irritated and chafed her and could not feel completely right.

Wasn't it old people who longed for peace and security and contentment? Wasn't it old people who wanted life to set in its mould with nothing threatening or unexpected around the corner? This North Yorkshire countryside called out to something young in her, and her memories, but didn't it also call out to something old, something placid, something that had long since ceased to surge and buck and laugh in people's faces?

Old and not yet twenty-five? When real life was supposed to be just beginning? Not yet, surely. Old was forty-five, when you realised how pointless and trivial the final effect of all that work had been. Or sixty-five when you perhaps had a right to demand peace and harmony even if you never got it. But twenty-five is not old.

Although it's not so young either.

Growing old is what happens to rock bands that start out exciting but then somehow become too sure of themselves and stop pushing and lose all the tension that made them so magnificent and become just boring and repetitive and slow and rich.

Growing old is what happens to bands that have just a few hits when they are nineteen or twenty, and then spend the rest of their lives playing second-rate cabarets and northern clubs on the strength of what they did almost by accident when they were fifteen years younger.

Growing old was the school hero-hooligan that you met in later life and found wearing a tie and going to work just like everyone else. It was when all the wild exciting things were memories, and you understood how kids felt because you had once been one yourself. It was when three-quarters of the performers on 'Top of the Pops' seemed younger than you.

And it was so seductive.

Maybe it was the straight kids, the ones who avoided fights, who never got into trouble, who never went to gigs that were the lucky ones. They went to college or got married, and then on to expanding companies or healthy families, and presumably felt no qualms. Unless the recession was having its effect on them too, the suckers.

You left the gigging behind you, and the drinking in slummy pubs. She had pretty well done that already, apart from her own gigs. You abandoned the constant effort to keep ahead of fashion. You did not so much ignore what belonged to the present as shift your values. You appreciated permanence, not newness, solidity and depth, not speed and superficial brightness. And you felt easier for it.

And society swallowed you up, and you became nervous

when you saw three or four youths together, and all your rock and roll/heavy metal/punk records were left unplayed and finally put away, and you stopped feeling angry so much of the time and you worried about 'practical' matters instead.

And you did this, or anyway, Alison did this, at twenty-four.

And if you did not, what were you? An out-of-date would-be hipster rattling off the names of bands you had never heard, trying to hide an ageing face beneath a Smash Hits haircut and the day before yesterday's ideas beneath yesterday's secondhand rhetoric.

Whatever way, you lose.

Alison stopped on a hillside on the other side of Thirlby, and looked back across the tranquil vale, even in the 1980s still unchanging, permanent, solid, gentle, where generation followed generation in an orderly peaceful succession, and all the fuss and fizz on the top was just so much pleasant sparkle.

It was where she belonged. It was what had made her what she was, deep inside. It was so old.

She did not want to know what happened to singers who grew old without even one hit single to lean their reputations on.

She pushed all that to one side, determined not to think about it. She was entering woods now, into the nature reserve that surrounds Lake Gormire. She walked all the way around the lakeside. It was not a large lake, and it had a funny air of getting there quite by accident, as if it did not really belong there at all. But it was peaceful. You could believe in tree spirits and water spirits here. You could believe that elves lived with the badgers and the foxes among the tree roots and that something from a fairy story could appear quite matter of factly right in front of you. Once, when she had been here as a child, she had found the low remains of a house, little more than an outline of raised grass. She looked for it now, but she had no real idea of where it was and so never found it. She would love to live here.

She tried to ignore the path that went up the hill, beneath Whitestone Cliff and up to the top of Sutton Bank. She clambered up through the trees and over a crumbling stone wall, and up through bracken and undergrowth, but became so hot and so tired, and the way above seemed so steep, that when she did cross the path she could only be glad. By way of apology it managed to make itself quite narrow and uneven in places, and she was able to feel she was still out in wild countryside despite the occasional route markers.

Beneath the scar of the cliff were huge sandy-coloured boulders, great blocks flat and wide enough for a family to picnic on. You stood on these and imagined them crashing down here centuries before. With the boulders beside her and the great cliff above her and the little valley with the lake behind her, it was like the scenery you saw in some adventure film.

The path moved sideways and upwards, and the lake with its guarding hillsides moved away behind you and you could look down into the vale, the ribbon of road, the tiny farm buildings, the red smudge of Thirsk off in the distance. It was wondrous. Every few yards she stopped to turn and stare.

She saw a dark shape fluttering furiously about yet staying perfectly in one place in the sky, and realised it was a kestrel, a windhover, the first she was ever conscious of seeing. It hung for a long minute. Even a kite caught at the end of its line could not stay so firmly placed. Then it dropped a few yards and hung again, wheeled about and hung again, and then suddenly it was off to hunt elsewhere.

She reached the top.

There seemed to be a lot of people up here. They parked their cars at the top of the bank, and walked along the path by the edge. It was a disappointment after such solitude. She could not even see an ice cream van by way of compensation. An ice cream would be welcome after such a climb.

She crossed the road and walked a good way along the path on the other side before she jumped down on to a wide, grassy ledge from which she could not possibly fall and where she could ignore the people passing behind her, and peeled her third orange.

She had hardly eaten it before a young girl came up behind her, saying, 'Hello, can I join you?' as she sat down.

'It's such an incredible view, don't you think?' the girl said, ignoring Alison's silence.

'Do you want an apple?'

Alison shook her head.

'Look, they're going to have rain in Thirsk.' Sure enough, there were clouds forming across the vale, with Thirsk right in their path.

'My name's Susan Oliver. What's yours?'

Alison told her.

'I used to live in Thirsk,' said Susan. 'Now I live in York. I'm training to be a model.'

She looked very young. She had thick, long, dark hair and large, dark eyes that were strikingly beautiful.

'Really?' said Alison. She finally took the offered apple. She was hungry.

'What about you? What do you do?'

'I'm . . .' There were problems with saying you were a singer. They inevitably ask if you have any records out, and then they say they've never heard of you.

'I'm thinking of becoming a nun,' she said, rather cynically.

'Yeh? I hate all that religious stuff.'

Alison felt amused, both at the girl's believing her and her honest response.

'Why is that?' she asked, keeping up the part.

'Oh . . . It's a cop-out, isn't it?'

'Why a cop-out?'

'I don't know. People who go into monasteries or become priests or whatever, they're saying sort of, "I'm all right, the rest's your problem." '

'I'm sure there are some orders that go out and help people.'

'Well, maybe, some. But it's still just a sort of escape, as far as I can see.'

'Yes,' said Alison. 'I suppose it is.'

'I mean, at least politicians, for example . . . Well, politicians are all in it for themselves anyway, but at least they actually do something, they aren't just going blissfully off after their own happiness.'

'What about models? That's just a sort of escapism. Or actors or singers?'

'Yeh, but they're making other people happy as well. Actors and singers, anyway. And models, too, because people like nice clothes and like to see them on beautiful women. And it could change things, too. Suppose it was possible, there were enough theatres and things, for anyone who wanted to be an actor or a singer to become one, for a living. That would make the world a better place because then you wouldn't have all these bored people in boring jobs being turned into pieces of wood.'

'That's a little unrealistic.'

'Yeh, all right. But suppose the Government gave unemployed kids the money to form bands or to set up theatres or dress shops or whatever. Just think of the results.'

'Bad music, bad plays, and bad dresses.'

'Well I don't know about *that,*' commented Susan, an edge to her voice. 'I don't know about that at all.'

They sat silent for a few minutes, staring out over the wide countryside beneath them. There was a track halfway down the hill, and they could see two splodges of bright clothes walking along it.

'I think,' Alison said, 'I think that all anyone wants is to be happy and do the things they most want to do. But generally people have to accept second best and make do, or third best and be horribly miserable. And if you've got second best, you've got to work as hard as you can to make it first best. Even if you don't succeed. And maybe the more people who try, the more people will be successful.'

'That sounds unrealistic to me. I mean, what about someone living in poverty in the Third World or wherever? Or under some oppressive dictatorship?'

'I don't know. People with far more time to waste than we have have come up with far cleverer arguments than we ever could. I don't think you can really talk about making people happy *en masse*. You get these political theorists and leftists who seem to think it's a shameful thing that people should try to be happy without first bringing about some worthless revolution. It's got to be individuals wanting to be happy. Not statistical groups and sociological theories and all that rubbish. I don't think that's escapism.'

'No, I suppose not.'

'And I don't think faith is just vapid saintliness and timid appeasement, either. Or it shouldn't be. Anymore than it should be narrow-mindedness and trivial dogma. It's finding the best in yourself and using that to meet the world on more equal terms. That's what faith means. That's not escapist, either.'

'Is that why you're going into a monastery?'

Alison laughed.

'I'm not,' she admitted. 'I just said that.'

'Oh.' Susan laughed too.

'Well what do you really do?'

'I'm . . . a singer.'

'Yeh? Do you have any records out?'

'A few. They haven't been all that successful, though.'

The girl was looking at her hard, trying to place her.

'What's your name, again?'

Alison told her, knowing what came next.

'I don't think I've ever heard of you. What sort of stuff do you do?'

'Oh, middle of the road, I suppose.'

'Oh. I never listen to Radio Two.'

Silence.

But it still wasn't really an answer. Perhaps it was not escapist, but surely it was a bit selfish. And how could you be truly saintly if all the time you were just being selfish? Maybe we are not expected to be saintly, but to do the best we can from day to day, neither saints nor sinners. It certainly did not seem like much to aspire to.

'Life is complicated,' Alison sighed.

Susan nodded her head sagely.

A bird swooped by them, faster and wilder than any bird you ever saw near the ground, high in full flight, completely uncaring about their grassy ledge. Enjoying a breather from scratching out a living, no doubt.

'Actually,' said Susan, 'I'm not really training to be a model.'

'No?' said Alison, amused. 'What are you really?'

'I'm not really anything. I'm in my last year at school.'

'What would you like to be?'

'I don't know. I don't want to go to college, I know that. There's lots of things I could be, really. Maybe painting or singing or, I don't know. I can do anything, I think.'

'It always seems like that. It's not so easy once you actually get started.'

'Yeh, I suppose not. What I'd really like to be is a dress designer like Vivienne Westwood.'

'Who?'

'Vivienne Westwood. You know, the Sex Pistols and all that.

I've got an interview with Vivienne Westwood in a 1977 *New York Rocker*. That's very rare. I'm the only person I know with a copy of *New York Rocker*. Most people don't even know it exists.'

'She designs punk clothes, does she?' The name was beginning to ring a bell from her own younger days.

'She used to. Now she's pirates and the Adam Ant style thing, although I don't like that so much.'

'You liked the punk stuff, did you?'

'Yeh. Although my mother never used to let me buy the records when they first came out. How come you sing the sort of stuff you do? Why don't you do something more interesting? I don't mean punk, just more interesting, you know?'

Alison shrugged, but her brow creased.

'You see so many fashions come and go, you lose interest after a while,' she said. 'It's more important to develop your own style, don't you think?'

'If I was a singer I'd be like Toyah. Or David Bowie. If I was a man I'd be like David Bowie. The first record I ever got was by David Bowie.'

'All that punk stuff,' said Alison, 'or mods or skinheads or rockers, it's just another sort of conformity. They're not really being different, they're just following the herd. The herd's just smaller, that's all.'

'You try being different all by yourself without being famous or having a bunch of friends who are different with you, and just see the trouble you'll get yourself into. Besides, when people have the same likes and dislikes, what's wrong with them sticking together and dressing the same? It's not following the herd. Not except for some nurd who twigs on to everything two years late and has to read the *NME* to find out what he's supposed to be thinking.'

'Is that what you read, the *NME*?' Alison used to read the *NME* faithfully every week.

'*NME*'s really boring these days. *Sounds* is better.'

'I've never read *Sounds*.'

Alone again, she wandered back along the cliff edge. She meant to follow her original path down to the lake, then another past a farm to the main road where she would wait for a bus. That way she would get back quicker (she was getting tired) and she would not have to retrace her original route all the way (very boring).

She was no longer paying much attention to the view, although she buttoned her coat against the gathering clouds and cold.

David Bowie, she knew, must be 'old'. It must be ten years since he had been Ziggy Stardust. Yet today he was no absurd self-parody. The quality of his work was more uneven, he often found it harder to have big hits, but he was still producing good material and still commanding a lot of respect.

How old was Debbie Harry now? How old was Nico, fifteen years ago just another Andy Warhol sidekick with a pretty face, now someone whose very name conjured up enigma and dark mysteries. No one pointed a finger when *her* records failed to reach the Top 40.

Growing older did not mean anything. Not necessarily. To think that was to confine yourself to a life of immaturity. Look at Beethoven. He actually got better as he grew older, more adventurous rather than less.

'It's stupid, all this thinking,' she thought. Thinking never really solved anything, not really solved, not this sort of thing anyway. The mind was like a pool, and all this threshing of thought was like so many active fish kicking up the mud and making it hard to see the bottom.

Old, young, permanence, change, this, that. It was the self that mattered. Being exclusively you. Exercising care and discrimination over all those things that shaped you, whether they were ageing and experience or managers and agents and promoters. It is a sort of integrity writ large that matters, and makes all that other darting activity seem quite inconsequential. It is looking in and seeing clearly that enables you to see clearly when looking out.

'Still . . .' she thought, stepping from the high moorland on to her path.

'Although . . .' beginning her descent.

'When you're only earning enough to live, and no one knows who you are, and if you did try to be modern and original people would just laugh and say you're clutching at straws and jumping on bandwagons . . . it's not easy.'

A squall of rain swept around her, but passed before she got too wet. The path would grow slippy if it got wet. She knew the slope was gentle and there were enough trees and undergrowth that she could not fall far. But she still tried to walk a little faster and a little more carefully so that she would get down quicker. With the weather turning bad she wished she had waited for the bus at the top of the bank. She wished she could just concentrate on the world around her without being constantly assailed by ALL THESE THOUGHTS.

Thirsk was wet when she reached it. She had seen the storm from a distance, had heard the thunder and seen the lightning, but she had been untouched.

Two hours later it was raining again, though not so badly, as she made her way to the church. Once more looking for a quiet piece of nostalgia but also, deeper down, seeking some sort of confirmation that what was timeless was also good, some affirmation of the unity of youth and maturity, so that the tempestuous, tempting years in the middle could be overlooked, set aside, put away.

She arrived five minutes late, but had no difficulty finding a seat. The church was nine-tenths empty. The choir – she clearly remembered the large choir of her childhood, twenty or more – was two old men and three old women. Not a person in the building could be under forty, save for herself and her curate/vicar.

Was this usual now? Surely it was the rain, or there was something else on that was keeping them away, or perhaps they all came in the mornings? Was it always like this? Did the Church of England, with its ancient rites and splendours, mean no more to these seven thousand honest healthy Yorkshire folk than it meant to her seven million heathen London compatriots? Was this the unity that bridged the aeons, this old folks' club, where white-haired gentlemen went through rituals of harmless mumbo-jumbo?

She listened to the sermon. It was a good sermon, he clearly had a way with anecdotes and stories. Yet, for all that, what was he doing? Morris dancing down the avenues of history, bells ringing, ribbons waving, formations precise, trying hard not to look embarrassed.

There was no consummation to be had here, that was certain.

Maybe nothing ever could be resolved. Maybe as soon as you grasp hold of the truth then the truth changes. Maybe just seeing your life changes your life, and the truth you saw no longer fully applies.

Maybe there is no truth. Just fashion.

She caught an early train the next morning, walking back to the station past girls who could once have been her, girls in her old school uniform, and was back in London before noon.

She called Bree when she got home.

'Hi,' said Bree, 'that was a short holiday. Anything up?'

'No, it was fine. Terry was saying he thinks I should make some changes in my show.'

'Hmmm. I think so too, really.'

'Why don't I come round, and we can go over it together?'

'Sure, kiddo. Hold on, let's see. Can you make it about 3.30?'

Anyway, thought Alison, as she hung up, she wouldn't starve.

RACIST FRIEND

One cloudless summer morning on his way to work Swank was stopped by a policeman. Swank had glanced at him as he passed by, noticing that he was black, but not really paying him any attention. As he stood waiting for the lights to change at the road he felt a hand on his shoulder and the policeman told him to come over to one side.

Swank frowned, but did so.

'I'd like your name and address, please.'

Swank wanted to know why.

'As I walked past you looked at me funny.'

Swank might have been tempted into some insulting retort, except that so early in the morning he did not feel at all up to hassles with the police.

'Oh yeh?'

The policeman said that the funny look he claimed to have seen could well indicate a guilty conscience.

'Would you have stopped me for a funny look if I'd been wearing a suit?' asked Swank.

The policeman started to explain that being black he was often himself the victim of just that sort of prejudice, but Swank only scowled. He knew why he had been stopped, because of his short hair and his boots, and because the policeman was black. No doubt the rookie had been gleefully awaiting this moment since the day he joined the force. Another policeman, white this time, joined them.

Swank gave his correct name but an old address. He could not think of anything serious that they could connect him with.

The black called in to the station on his radio. He seemed to have some trouble with it, and then when he got through he had an unusually long delay while the person at the other end got him his answer. Swank stood raging, but totally silent, not helping the man out of his growing embarrassment and not doing anything to give them an excuse to jump on him. The black was beginning to think he might have been wrong, and the white policeman, not having any idea what it was about, made casual conversation with his fellow to try to ease the tension. Two black youths stood on the corner, watching and grinning.

Finally the answer came through that there was no reason to hold him, and they told him he could go. The black started to explain again and to apologise, but Swank ignored him and stalked away, cold with fury.

At work Phil said, 'Now suppose you'd been black and he'd been white. The Race Relations people would have been slobbering all over you.' He raised his voice an octave and waved his hands in the air. 'Racist oppression! Racist oppression!'

Swank said nothing. But he clearly believed Phil to be right.

Swank at this time was working as a house painter. He was a much more contained person than he used to be, his former impulsive pugnacity reined in, and all the harder for being the more controlled. Because he no longer so angrily demanded that things work out in his favour he was not as ready to hit out in frustration when they did not. But when he did hit out it was with vicious glee because he knew exactly what he was doing and accepted the consequences. People found him harder to get to know than they had once done.

Phil said, 'They scream racial prejudice and all the fucking media are crawling at their feet wanting to take down every word they say. They go and burn down half the city and the Government comes along and gives them a big grant as a reward. We're fucking hooligans if we just walk along the street, and if we've got problems it's "Tough luck, mate, get to the back of the queue." '

Phil saw the violence in Swank, just beneath the surface, but resented the control, taking it for mere apathy.

Swank pulled the covering off the cans of paint and unwrapped the brushes. 'Yup,' he said.

When he got home he found Sally wandering about wrapped in her winter coat, for all it was the middle of summer. She had soft blonde hair, so fine and delicate there was no way to disguise the bald patches where it kept falling out. Her skin clung to her tiny bones, she seemed on the verge of starvation. The pupils of her eyes sparkled large in shadowed hollows. This constant glitter, giving her a look of barely repressed insanity, was what had attracted Swank to her in the first place. He had adopted her like a tramp would adopt a stray dog, for mutual comfort and for something to be superior to.

'Hiya, baby,' she said in the American twang she sometimes affected. 'How ya doing?'

She lit a cigarette and drew on it stylishly, as if she was in a thirties movie. Then, after she had been Mae West for a few minutes, she stopped abruptly and turned to him with alarm on her face.

'Are you wanting dinner?'

He nodded. She threw off her coat and hurried to the kitchen, full of apologies for keeping him waiting.

Swank put an album on, and settled down to look through *The Times* she bought faithfully every morning.

Over the very acceptable dinner she said, 'Do you think I should take yoga? I've been thinking of taking yoga.' She showed him a circular the local council had put out about night school classes. 'It says I can take yoga lessons right close by here, at the school. £16 for two terms, September to May. Do you think I should?'

'Why not?' said Swank.

'I don't know, though,' she mused, leafing through the circular. 'They have motor mechanics. If I learnt about motor mechanics we could get a car.'

A pause, then, 'I heard something about your friend Carrie today.'

'Did you?' Not wanting to show too much interest.

'But I'm not telling you what I heard.' Stubborn resentment rather than coquetry.

'Fine.'

A short while ago Swank had been seeing a girl in New Addington. Sally had found out about it and had got her revenge by breaking into the girl's flat, stealing all her spoons, and cutting all the buttons off her clothes. Then she had come back to Swank's flat, scattered spoons and buttons liberally over floor and furniture, and taken overdoses of whatever she could lay her hands on.

'Don't you want to know?' she said, thwarted.

'Can't be much if it's not worth telling.'

'Well I'll tell you. She's going away. Back to Yorkshire. So you'll never see her again.'

She watched Swank for his reaction, but he only went on with his chips.

'Well I say good riddance to her.' And feeling more satisfied she went to make the tea.

Swank switched on the TV at random and came upon a noisy demo. A man in a suit was shouting, 'Britain for the British! Throw out the foreign invaders!' It took him some minutes to realise the demonstrators were leftists and the foreign invaders were the Americans.

Greatly entertained, he changed channels.

After they finished the South Croydon job painting renovated cottages, the boss sent them down to Chipstead on the fringe of Surrey, where some people in big houses wanted their doors and window-frames repainted.

Swank had been unhappy about the idea of getting a job, had only done so because he was fed up with life as it was. In the normal way he would have had very little chance, but Phil was an old mate, he had recommended Swank to the boss, and Swank had been taken on almost sight unseen. The boss had three or four small teams doing jobs at various houses. He called on each of them once a day, and as long as they were getting on with it he left them pretty much to their own devices.

Swank had never done anything of this kind before, but found it easy enough. After he had put the paint on too thinly and then too thickly, and after he had fallen off the ladder, and after he had got his work clothes proudly speckled and spattered, he began to settle into it and even to enjoy it. He started to wonder what he had found so great about constant idleness. He soon learnt just how little sleep he really needed, and so with more money in his pockets his social life was better than ever. Having a hangover seemed to have no effect at all on his ability to paint.

Just down the street was a village pub overlooking a gunge-strewn village pond, and they used to go there and sit out in the sun at lunchtimes. Phil was in the National Front, having given up the British Movement as 'a bunch of louts'. Although he talked about lots of other things, it was the politics that stuck in your mind. Because often he seemed to make sense. Sometimes he was crude and bigoted and emotional. But sometimes Swank felt he had put his finger right on the problem.

'You're not supposed to talk to me because of that,' Phil once said. 'That's why the Left want people like us ostracised. They're scared that if people start to talk to us they'll start to listen.'

Swank said, dubiously, 'How do you get rid of five million blacks? Secret police? Concentration camps?'

'A lot of them would be glad to leave if they were given the money,' Phil said. 'Who can blame them? There's lots of whites would take Jamaican sunshine to British winters.' Then, swinging wildly back into rhetoric, 'Besides, they'd do the same to us if they had the chance.'

'I'll tell you something,' said Swank, 'one of the earliest memories I have is of a revolt in Africa that I saw on the News, and all these blacks were raging through the streets shouting, "Kill! Kill!" and setting fire to the whites' homes. And my mother was saying that's what would happen here if they let all those blacks in. And that was years before Enoch Powell did his rivers of blood bit. I'd forgotten all about that till now.'

'Everyone was against it. Everyone. Except for some well-off liberals with guilty consciences about not being born poor and black.'

'My grandmother used to be in the National Front as well,' said Swank.

'Your grandmother! Go on!' Phil laughed. 'Well, there you are. It runs in the family.'

'Yeh, but I'm not like them, am I? I'm not going to be like them in any way. Not if I can help it.'

'I'll tell you something,' said Phil. 'There's others have got backgrounds just like yours, except they don't admit it, not even to themselves. And they're the ones rushing around banning Noddy books and jam-jar labels. They're scared that deep down they might find that they agree with us.'

Swank said, 'I remember there was this neighbour emigrating to Canada, and I was at their house when the news was on TV and there were all these Asians piling off the planes, and they were saying how they were glad they were leaving if that was what was happening.'

Two women, housewives, wandered in comfortable ease along the path to the children's playpark, one of them holding the hand of a pretty little girl in a check frock.

'If you love this land,' Phil said, 'then you want it to be there for your children. That's the real issue. Who inherits England? The English? The blacks? The Pakis? Or some bastardised hybrid?

'You listen to what the Left is saying,' he went on. 'They hate England. They think the English are an ugly jingoistic rabble. The only whites they approve of are the IRA and the Russians.'

Swank and Sally went to a gig at a college in central London. The band was a Rough Trade band that Swank and Carrie had gone to see quite often when they first arrived in the city. Nowadays Swank tended to dislike Rough Trade signings, but he thought he would go along just for old times' sake.

The doors were late in opening of course, and they stood out in the street, listening to people talk. Swank was trying to suss out the source of the strange atmosphere colleges always have, but Sally's eye was caught by the motorbikes lined up at the kerb.

'You think we should get one, do you?' Swank asked.

'A big one,' she said. 'Brand new.'

Swank grinned, confident in his new-found wealth. 'Yeh, all right.'

'Is that a promise?' asked Sally.

Swank agreed. It was a promise.

Sally looked over the bikes with a new appraising attention.

'I should have brought a crash helmet with me,' she said.

Once inside there was a further wait, right up against the

stage, Swank's favourite position. They each had a pint, and with four extra cans they had enough to keep them going through to the end. They turned round to look at the crowd until something should happen onstage. Just behind them was a girl with a dwarf. The dwarf had curly Latin hair and a full moustache. He dressed like a high-ranking hood, his solid grey coat with its severe cut and its square shoulders emphasising rather than disguising his ungainly bulk. He looked so determinedly macho, so deliberately mini-mafioso, that any tendency Swank and Sally had to smile was quickly hidden. He smoked a big cigar and strutted about like the most important man in the hall. His girlfriend was obviously well used to him, but her friend was finding it hard to resist gushing all over the dear little creature, which the dwarf stoically chose not to notice.

But the rest of the audience Swank found repulsive. It was the whole élitist-super cool-trendy axis. Serious young men with glasses and precisely the right shade of shabbiness to their cloth jackets, feminist women with larger glasses and ratty masculine haircuts. The DJ played fifties jive and Ray Charles type blues of the kind Swank had hated since he could walk, and the dowdy, socially aware young men and women, who despised HM for being unoriginal and punk for being old fashioned, slapped their hands together and beamed broadly. It was, after all, the only legitimate form of popular music, as opposed to disco-funk or whatever had been the only legitimate form of popular music the year before, or New Wave before that, or progressive rock before that. They summed up all the people who had betrayed him, all the hip sheep who had dumped punk for salsa and the bossa nova, and done it in the name of *rebellion.*

Swank had his own opinions on why they elevated this ancient black music to such heights. It was because it had to be black, and most modern black music was sterile, polished dross. When someone proclaimed to him that all rock was just black music watered down by the poor rhythmless soulless whites it made him want to drive a knife into their ribs. Someone had once told him that because he did not like jazz-funk that proved he was racist. Actually they had got cause and effect the wrong way round. All these hip young intelligentsia jumping about to Hit The Road Jack added extra weight to every word Phil spoke.

Other than that, however, he quite enjoyed himself.

Sally said, 'Which band did you like best?' and when he told her, she liked that band best as well. She was generally prepared to accept anything, Bucks Fizz, Pink Floyd or Vice Squad, and her opinions of the moment invariably depended on who she was with. Sometimes Swank envied her for it.

Sally decided not to take yoga after all, and they went down to look at motorbikes. The flat began to get cluttered up with Motorhead albums and studded leather wristbands – she bought them compulsively whenever she saw them. Meals became increasingly meaty, juicy steaks replacing frozen beef and kidney pies, and Swank was being regularly pestered to outfit her top to toe in black leather.

But they never got around to actually buying the bike because Swank was suddenly laid off. The boss had been over-reaching himself, some people had been slow in paying, he was not getting in all the business he needed. Three workers had to go, and it was last in, first out. There was even some worry about Swank getting his final week's pay.

Sally felt devastatingly betrayed. Swank offered to get a cheaper bike secondhand, but she would have none of it. She had had her heart set on something big and new and shiny, and driving it fresh out of the salesroom. She pouted endlessly, meals became reduced to the lightest essentials haphazardly thrown together, and she spent much of the time locked in the bedroom refusing to speak. A single heavy blow could have broken one of those tiny fleshless arms, and it was all Swank could do to keep from giving it.

But Sally was no more than a prickly irritation. The real weight of Swank's troubles came from being thrown back on the dole. The clockwork mechanism that delivered him his Giro once every two weeks had been disrupted by his brief absence from the list of suppliants. The DHSS had become consciously aware of his existence, had turned its heavy eyes upon him, and was pawing him about to see if there was anything it could do to him. Finally, after keeping him waiting in several different offices over three different days, it decided to acquiesce, and Swank was told his money would arrive as before.

It didn't.

He went up to find out why, and a girl behind a glass screen told him he had been put on hold for three weeks due to some sin or error. When he wanted to know what sin or error, he was sent off to another building two miles away. Here there was a gloomy waiting-room with some fifty chairs for those with questions and three service windows for those with answers. On the wall was a spool of numbered tickets. Swank took a ticket, number seventy-two. The indicator indicated that they were presently serving number thirty-four. Only one window was occupied.

On a table was a suggestion box.

Four hours later his number was called and he was told it had all been a mistake and his money would arrive in a couple of days.

It did. £30 short.

He went back to see them, getting there early this time and so cutting the waiting to two hours and twenty-five minutes. His benefit money, he was told, now excluded his rent money which would come from his local council and should arrive in a couple of days.

It didn't. But he still had some money in hand, so he left it for a while trusting that the wheels of bureaucracy would produce it soon enough.

They didn't. Nor did they produce his next dole cheque.

He went back to see them, this time being told, 'Can't understand it. Our mistake . . . will arrive in a couple of days.' Then he went to the local council offices to find out about the rent money and was told, '. . . inevitable delays, staff shortages. No problem, be with you in a couple of days.'

He and Sally sat at home every night watching TV and growling at each other. On Friday there was going to be a row with the landlord about not being able to pay the rent.

Meanwhile he read in the paper that Hackney Council were reserving some jobs especially for blacks. He switched on the radio and heard a Government minister talking about how every effort had to be made to solve the problems of blacks. He switched on the TV where a black woman was talking about how tough the blacks had it in Birmingham and how terrible it was being black in Britain.

When Swank went looking for a job and got nowhere despite his two months' experience as a painter, when he was turned down enough times that he ceased to bother and slipped discontentedly back into his old habits, he could not go pleading the colour of his skin as an excuse. Nor did he need an overwhelming amount of bigotry to start subtracting five million immigrants from three million unemployed and come to some conclusions about just who was being done.

His dole money began to arrive regularly again, and his anger eased as the financial alarms were stilled. But it was not forgotten. He met Phil in the street and they went for a drink.

'Thing is,' Swank said, 'you're not going to get anywhere because no matter how many people think they shouldn't have been let in, lots of people now have one or two black friends and buy Michael Jackson and Diana Ross records. Every person who ever collected Tamla Motown and every kid that dances to soul and funk at the local disco is a vote against you.'

'So we fight all the harder. We let people know the truth. You should see some of the fucking big houses that are owned by blacks and Pakis that we see when we're painting, the poor oppressed little bastards. Besides, wait till there's a few more riots and people start getting killed. The blacks will do our work for us.'

Phil pressed him to go to a meeting, although Swank could not really be bothered. Phil gave him a leaflet to read when they parted. It seemed to Swank like a ragbag of leftist ideas such as leaving NATO tagged on to the usual, 'Wogs out!' He gave it to Sally to read and she declared herself confused. But she sat down to puzzle it out point by point, and Swank saw with some amusement that she was beginning to be converted.

She was a true follower, a dedicated believer. The Moonies or Jehovah's Witnesses, the Anti-Blood Sports League or a subscription to *Horse and Hound*, you could convert her to anything if you got her undivided attention for long enough.

But Swank was not willing to consider himself as fodder for political cannons and had no intention of being converted to anything. He felt betrayed in this too, betrayed by all his contemporaries who had proudly declared their independence of politics, Left or Right, but who now spouted leftist rhetoric as ugly as anything he had ever heard. They went to the meeting.

The event had been publicised solely by word of mouth, no advertising at all. If it got out where and when it was, the Left would arrive and try to bust it up. They would cause noise and damage, get the police involved, and then their friends on the Council would have further meetings banned on the grounds that they lead to violence.

But despite the precautions, they were met by a dozen demonstrators with placards and baseball bats. They had parked a van across the main door and had suggested to the caretaker that he take himself and his keys home to his family if he did not want to get himself into trouble.

Swank grinned, feeling the old urge for action welling up inside him. Although he had to keep a close eye on Sally who was not up to any fighting yet was none the less getting carried away with outrage.

There were about twenty NF supporters, some of whom had brought their own weapons in the hope of a ruck. Their organiser, a small, close-faced man in a sweater, was trying to cool things down and to reason with the demonstrators. He had got his supporters to place small 'Vote NF' stickers all over town, and they did not need this sort of reputation if people were going to take any notice.

Swank read some of the placards. 'Class War Not Race War' said one, which he thought pretty good given the background of the likes of Tony Benn. Another said, 'Jobs, Equality, Freedom', to which Swank added an ironical, 'For Who?'

And of course the Church was there. A priest in full black drag who stood with his arms folded, his face determined. On either side of him white youths howled and brandished clubs.

Taunts became scuffles. Phil was involved in a screaming match. His opponent was white, was not well-dressed, was not well-off, and clearly had more than enough troubles of his own. What was it, Swank wondered, that got him so twisted with rage about the one problem that did not directly affect him – being black? If they had been met by a crowd of stern-faced, working-class blacks Swank would have understood it. But the blacks were in the minority here, and looked if anything the better fed.

Some of the demonstrators set about the car of a Front supporter with their clubs, and a general punch-up broke out. Sally was taking kicks at a weedy student type but Swank grabbed her by the waist and pulled her away. It was not their fight. Politics and politicians disgusted him – he was not going to get himself knocked about on their behalf.

Police sirens were heard in the distance, and Swank and Sally took off down the nearest side street.

When they got home one of the free local tabloids was in the letterbox. On page four was a story about how two white youths had been stabbed outside a hamburger shop by a gang of thirty blacks. The white kids did not know any of the blacks, had done nothing to provoke them. All they wanted was a couple of hamburgers. Both survived but both were severely wounded.

Swank read it, shaking with anger. Because sooner or later, he was certain, someone was going to stand up and say that of course what those blacks did was wrong, but given the pressures they were under in racist Britain the occasional explosion was inevitable. And all thirty of them would be back roaming the streets while the two white guys were still in hospital.

He searched through the other free tabloids, and was not surprised when neither of them even mentioned the incident. It made him wish he'd stayed to fight it out with the leftists.

He tore out the article and kept it, as a reminder, and the next night he went over to Phil's place and they put their heads together.

There was a community centre in Thornton Heath that was mostly frequented by blacks. It had a good-sized hall for table tennis and snooker and the like, and at the back a snug little lounge with comfy furniture, a cheap stereo and an old fridge. The place was no more than reasonably secure. Phil and Swank swore they would pay it a visit.

They waited till the early hours of the morning, parked Phil's car a good ten minutes' walk from the hall, and let themselves in. The sports equipment was easy prey. There was enough light from the street to see by, and it did not take much to smash the lock to the cupboard. The game of snooker, in particular, suffered a severe setback.

Swank left all that to Phil. He had learnt enough by now not to go wasting all his frustrations on simple brute force. He made his way through to the back and calmly switched on the light.

There was a fat and friendly couch with three fat and friendly mismatched armchairs. He took off the cushions and slashed the seats, then he slashed the undersides of the cushions and put them back in place so nothing would show. He took out his screwdriver and worked the turntable off the stereo so he could get busy on the insides. He took out the stylus and threw it away, then set the playing arm back on its rest and replaced the turntable. Nor did he simply smash the records. He had supplied himself with three large round candles, which he had lit straight away. When the wax was pooling in little hollows around the wick he took the records out of their covers one by one, poured the wax over them, let it set, then put them neatly back in their place. There were magazines and paperbacks on the coffee-table and on a bench. He took out glue and superglue, stuck all the pages together, then glued books and magazines firmly to each other and to the wood. He switched off the fridge, got into the works, whistling between his teeth, and set about with screwdriver and pliers. He put the best of the drink to one side to take away with them and poured the rest down the drain, putting the empty cans and bottles back just as he had found them.

When Phil came in after finishing up on the sports equipment he could not see that the place had been touched and wanted to know what Swank had been doing all this time.

Swank laughed, his eyes narrow and glittering. 'We can't hang about,' he said. 'Someone might check on the lights.'

They got out the way they got in and drove back to Phil's place, cruelly imagining the shocks awaiting the club's regulars. Swank felt quite certain that all the local tabloids would make much of *this* little incident. They shared out the drink, then Swank kipped down on Phil's couch for the rest of the night.

Swank did not get home till late in the afternoon. The first thing he saw was a black guy coming out of the door of his flat.

Sally was beside him, her hand resting possessively on his arm, dressed in the old coat she used as a dressing-gown.

She saw Swank first, her face stricken, then defiant. The black backed away, wary but, it seemed, with a gleam of triumph in his eye. There is no better way to be revenged upon your enemies than to fuck their women. He turned and fled down the back stairs, but Swank ignored him, it was Sally he wanted. She tried to slam the door in his face, but he forced it open and shoved her across the room. When he approached her she threw up her arms in terrified defence, but all he did was rip off her coat and tell her to get dressed.

She had very few possessions. Swank found two large cardboard boxes and threw her things into them. As he strode about gathering up her worldly goods Sally, fully clothed again, taunted him to provoke a fight, pounded him with her fists, and wept and declared he did not love her.

He put her and the boxes out on the landing and told her not to come back. Subdued and tearful, she gathered them up and limped away.

He hoped she was gone for good. Her skin-and-bones body, her infantile ways, her dependency, they all made his stomach turn.

Not for the first time, and certainly not for the last, he wished he knew what had become of Carrie.

CARRIE

Carrie was reclining lazily in the bath one warm night in August. Both air and water were hot and wet, but while the water was grey with washed-off soap the air had a golden glow to it, given off by the light bulb, as if its molecules were those of honey rather than oxygen and steam and all the rest.

Her hydrotherapy had brought her to that calm, unthinking state when all personal ills seem very resolvable or very small, when the ferocity of thought is smoothed out and the brain seems to take on a comforting furriness, as if protected by downy feathers.

Hours or even years later, she reluctantly stood up and reached for the towel. She noticed a curious something in the air, like gathering thunderclouds. Sometimes, if you have an upper room with wide prospects, you can see a storm sweep up on you at night, magnificent and dazzling even in the distance, shattering when it is all around you, throwing itself against the house as if it knows you're there and would like to make some brief contact with your lesser being before it rushes on.

Carrie dried herself precisely. To be absorbed in the power of gathering wholly imaginary thunderclouds while standing dripping in several inches of bath water was to indulge in the first symptoms of a loosening mind.

She hung up the towel, put on some slippers and a T shirt, and wandered out into the main room, trying to decide if she should listen to a record.

Instantly the whirlwind struck her. There was a furious rushing of wings, a great wind careering about her that stirred neither curtains nor papers yet roared at her from all directions, making her heart beat and her skin prickle, a rolling Jovian phraseless voice that bore into her and forced her to the floor, gasping.

The pleasure of it was like being turned to warm, scented wine. Over her skin it flowed, in through the pores, filling her up and making her glow, causing her back to arch, her breasts to tingle, her teeth to be bared, while the wind, the great rushing wind, filled her soul and took from her all thought but of itself.

Some mighty presence spoke to her in words she did not know and could not afterwards recall. It filled the whole room, it seemed to shake the whole building, it seemed as if all down the street people must be fleeing panic struck from the great chasms opening in the road. Her spirit was sent dazed and ecstatic by the holy storm, swept along helplessly at its centre. She did not know self or anything else until gently, slowly, it withdrew and she was alone again, curled up beneath the table.

She got to her feet and staggered off to bed. Oh the ecstasy. Body and mind still felt overflowing with flavoured warmth. She wanted to hug herself, or jump or sing or cry or fuck. Or none of these things because none of them was equal to what she had just experienced. She lay down and fell into blissful sleep.

Not so very long after that she packed her things, gave up her flat, and got the train north to York.

The room that Carrie found through an ad in the *Evening Press* was in a tiny, ancient street almost at the centre of the city. The street was full of shops and flowing with traffic and people, but even so there was barely room for a good-sized horse and cart. Between a restaurant that boasted the excellence of its beef and a furniture shop displaying solid, dark-grained wood was an inconspicuous door that should have led to an office. You rang the bell, and if Anna was not in a foul mood she came clattering down the stairs to let you in.

She was perhaps thirty-five, with the intelligent, arresting face of the career woman, yet with the long dark hair and still supple slimness of someone much younger.

'I hope you can manage for yourself,' she said, for her work on that same *Evening Press* kept her out at irregular hours. She was giving Carrie the critical once-over, but expecting such problems Carrie had smoothed down her hair and dressed as conservatively as she knew how.

It was a small room, blandly furnished but well enough supplied with the usual creature comforts, more, in fact, than Carrie was used to.

'It looks fine,' she said.

Anna listened carefully to Carrie's explanation about the dole and housing benefits, and demanded the usual week's deposit and a week in advance. She told her she did not take kindly to boisterous parties and that Carrie would be expected to provide most of her own food.

It was a grim little lecture, suggesting the possibilities of the temperature here getting very chilly. But Carrie looked at Anna and suspected there was softer stuff underneath. Anyway, she had no wish to drag about the city looking for somewhere else.

'Fine,' she said, and paid the required amount.

Anna smiled, more relaxed now that business was done. 'I've got to go out, but you can find something to eat in the kitchen if you want.'

Carrie nodded and threw her jacket on to the bed. She heard Anna rushing about, then heard the door close and the sound of her shoes on the stairs. The street door slammed and she was on her own.

There was a living-room, a locked door which was presumably Anna's, and a kitchen. It was all done up in the same bland but comfortable middle-class style. The late summer light shone in through the window and the clock ticked peacefully. She could hear the cars in the street. It was either going to be nicely restful here or very dull.

She went into the kitchen and made herself a cup of tea. A framed colour photo of a Greek temple hung above the cooker.

With most of the afternoon still left and nothing much else to do, she put on her jacket again and went for a walk about the city. After London the shopping centre seemed absurdly small. There was a medieval quaintness to the place of a kind she had wholly forgotten and which London had long since lost. She still had no idea why on earth she had come here. It had not made her feel any less aimless.

That night Anna made dinner for both of them, declaring

meanwhile that they would have to work something out for cooking and cleaning.

Carrie nodded, sitting at the table, with nothing much to say.

'So you've come from London?' Anna asked, trying to encourage conversation.

'I used to live in Yorkshire before,' Carrie admitted.

'Yes, I noticed it in your accent.'

Anna found it hard-going. Carrie seemed taciturn, uninterested. The key to unlock her, conversationally, seemed for the moment to be missing.

'You just got bored of London?'

'Oh, just, you know . . .' Carrie could hear how tired and perfunctory she sounded, even worse than she often felt. Anna would think her dull or unfriendly, would have second thoughts about letting her live here. '. . . things.'

Anna filled the silence by making them some coffee, with an air of not quite knowing what else to do. Afterwards they went into the living-room to watch TV. There was a comedy series on BBC and they watched that, both of them for the first time. It was reasonably funny. Anna was thinking she would rather be reading a good book, but believed that when Carrie relaxed more she would open up a bit, and dutifully felt she should make the effort.

Carrie was wondering if she was going to end up spending all her nights here with Anna watching inane comedies on TV. She felt like a guest. To escape to her room seemed an impossible discourtesy.

She said, 'I think I'll go to my room.'

'All right,' said Anna, much relieved.

The door to Carrie's room closed and Anna frowned unhappily at the TV set. She had rented out the room hoping for companionship. She seemed to have lumbered herself with nothing but a moody, uncomfortable lodger. She supposed she should have known better.

She switched off the television and reached for her book.

The next day Carrie went looking for music and someone to talk to. She knew well enough, really, why she felt so miserable these days. Jobless, manless, directionless. No doubt she had come here simply seeking a change of scene, a fresh stimulation.

It was just a question of keeping her eyes open, exploring a little, finding new channels.

A mimeographed leaflet in a record shop directed her to a local musicians' collective organising weekly gigs at a pub, and she went there that Thursday night to check it out.

It was a normal, slightly dowdy pub. All the action was in a room at the back with black walls and a tiny stage. It was warm and ill-lit and friendly and everyone seemed to know everyone else. Two girls were at a table collecting the money, both outrageously blonde, confident undamaged faces at the centre of vast auras of blondness. They smiled at Carrie as they gave her her ticket, and said hello.

She sat down on another table at the back of the room and two men came and sat beside her, one on each side, both with an air of wanting to eat her up. Each was in a different band. The light-haired one was the more casual, but the dark-haired one had a clear streak of callousness to his intensity that in other times would have made her want to claw him down. She chatted away happily, building herself up, talking about London and the bands she had seen and the things she had done. The dark one lightly touched her back and shoulders every time he made a point. She saw a pair of youths over by the wall eyeing her moodily, and her happiness increased. This was better, she could make something of this.

His name was Den, and his band was playing here tonight. He was the guitarist.

'I love the guitar,' she said. 'Bands that aren't guitar-based just don't have any guts to them.'

'We've got guts,' said Den.

There were half-a-dozen people in the band, and several others who seemed to come on to play an instrument or sing along only in one or two songs. There was a girl keyboard player with an instrument done out in red plastic so that it looked like a toy.

And they were dire. They had lifted every note from the early seventies. Not the Ziggy-Bolan seventies, but the strictly-albums-but-not-too-experimental-only-doing-a-job-chief seventies, stolid and heavy-footed music that once started in a particular direction was unable to alter its course or emphasis until it reached the bitter end. The voices made it even worse, the lead singer rasping, the girl shrieking away on top of him. Carrie could not guess what Den had been so proud about.

'They're amazing,' said the light-haired one, still sitting beside her. 'They're such an amazing band.'

Yet she joined them at their table afterwards, lied when asked her opinion, and when it was time to go she went with them; she and Den and the bass player in a car, most of the others in a van with the equipment.

'We're in a band too, you know,' the two blondes told her, climbing into the back of the car. 'Except we're much better than them.'

Home seemed to be a large, old house at the top of a hill. They tumbled down the area steps into the basement. Den had his arm around her and took her on a tour. There were four or five bedrooms and a practice room, most of the band seemed to live here and those that didn't might as well have. Den's room had a mattress on the floor and huge posters on the walls – the posters a bizarre mix of sixties psychedelia and eighties Crass . . . or not so bizarre when you think about it. There were literally yards of albums stacked along the walls.

Den was filling a pipe.

'Switch off the top switch and switch on the one beneath it,' he instructed.

The top switch engulfed them in darkness, the bottom one illuminated them again with black light.

She wondered how old he really was.

Den got the pipe lit. She sniffed at the smoke and smelt only straight marijuana.

'Here, sit down,' he said. They sat on the mattress and he passed her the pipe.

Someone outside was saying, 'Where's Den?' and a voice shouted 'Den!' He reached up and locked the door before they started banging on it, wanting him to help unload the van. Finally they gave up, and the two of them snuggled down into the pillows.

He kissed quite nicely. But unlike Swank, who was demanding but somehow open and direct about it, in Den she felt again that hard callousness, as if all he thought he was doing was pushing buttons to get her to respond in the way he wanted.

She forced herself to blank out all the things she didn't like about him, and let her thoughts sink deliciously into her body.

She turned up at Anna's the following afternoon and made herself a pot of tea.

'Hello there,' said Anna, coming into the kitchen. 'A cup of tea feels just about right. I've been working all day on that bloody article.' She thought that her house-guest looked more cheerful for her night out. She poured herself a cup.

'So what did you get up to last night?' Hoping she did not sound as if she were interrogating.

Carrie could not have cared less about Anna's article. If she played her cards right she could get out of here and live with the band. 'Went to see a band. Met some friends.'

'People you used to know up here?'

'No. A bloke in the band.' She felt sorry for Anna, living alone here, unconnected with the real rhythms of the city despite her job on the newspaper. 'They're not that brilliant,' honesty compelled her to admit, 'but . . .'

Later, in her room, she asked herself, but what? But they're all that's going? But they're better than nothing? But they fill a desperate void?

If she did not keep a grip on things she could end up like Anna. Despite still looking pretty good Anna seemed to have moved firmly into the world of the middle-aged, without even picking up the middle-age consolations of home and family. Den must be as old as Anna, but he hadn't let himself give in like that. Stay involved, stay in touch, or who knew where she might drift? She had drifted too long already.

They passed in the lounge as she left, Carrie looking decidedly scruffier than she had ten minutes before, as if she had set to and unpolished herself.

'I might be back tonight,' she said. 'I don't know.'

The door slammed. She was gone. Anna took in the silence.

'What else did you expect?' she asked herself, rather disappointed. She knew very well what she had expected, or hoped anyway. She went back to her typing.

Besides, she was a very busy person, and a live-in friend, as opposed to a lodger, would demand and deserve a great deal of time. She would be prepared to give that time, of course, but just at the moment, with work as it was . . .

She went back to her typing.

One of the blondes answered the doorbell, the little orangey blonde not the more stream-lined silvery blonde. Maybe she should grow her hair out like them, be the golden blonde. Everyone seemed pleased to see her. The band were just settling down to some practising. Den had switched on a tape of last night's set, and he and the singer were listening to it intently. The girl keyboard player, Carrie noticed again, looked surprisingly straight both in her clothes and her hair, quite apart from her failings as a vocalist. But she had seen that the girl and the singer had both emerged from the same bedroom that morning, so perhaps that explained it.

She noticed also that neither of the two blondes seemed at all interested in watching the practice.

'I think I'll make a cup of tea,' she announced, and wandered out into the truncated kitchen, closing the door behind her. They'd think she'd never seen a band practise before if she hung around listening to every bum note. And you could hear them just as well through the walls.

'Oh God look at this fucking heel,' said the silvery blonde, trying to see why she was suddenly walking funnily then kicking off both shoes. 'You haven't seen some biscuits have you?'

That night, in bed, she told Den all about Swank and how he had walked out on her and how miserable she had been.

'Not just 'cos of Swank,' she tried to explain. 'Not just 'cos of him. Things . . . Like, everything's always being eaten away. Like a brick wall, as soon as you build it, it starts to crumble. You can't leave anything alone without its falling apart behind your back. There's nothing you can count on in this life. There's nothing that just *is*, of itself. Everything keeps running down, everything keeps demanding you to put more and more into it just so it will stay almost as good as it was the day before. I hate all that. It's pointless, really, mostly.'

Den had been very sympathetic. Under the circumstances you would expect him to be sympathetic. While he was being sympathetic he was stroking her breasts, his mind clearly on things other than what she said.

Carrie abandoned thought for action. It's thinking about things that gets you depressed.

The next day Den and the singer had a giggle over how Carrie had been explaining to him the second law of thermodynamics in bed.

Carrie visited Anna's flat only briefly in the following days, a quick in and out to change her clothes and to pick up or return some small possession, make-up and so forth. Sometimes Anna was in, sometimes not, it made no real difference to her. Anna these days figured very little in Carrie's idea of what was important. In fact, with her friendly hellos and goodbyes she felt she was exercising remarkable civility, considering all the woman had to do was collect her rent and then not see her for another day or two. Ten, five minutes and she was gone.

Anna said hello and goodbye and put all her thoughts, as ever, into her job. Anna saw a lot of people in the course of her work, she brushed against a lot of lives. She was able to listen to what people had to say and make sympathetic sense of it.

Men often tried to draw Anna out, attracted by her intelligence and good looks. But the ones that she felt as if she could have trusted if they had tried to take things further were precisely the ones that were intimidated by her rock hard self-sufficiency, and those that were not intimidated were generally the very ones she did not feel able to trust.

There were occasions when Anna wanted to tighten up her fists and simply smash everything.

But mostly she got along pretty nicely.

Carrie, too, was getting along pretty nicely with the band, fitting into the flow of things, learning who was what, which ideas and which people were held in high regard and which were derided. She discovered that the drummer had Airfix model aircraft hanging from the ceiling of his room and was a sucker for old war films. She assimilated the songs without even being wholly aware of it, and if she was still no great enthusiast their failings were no longer so very obvious to her. She swapped clothes and thoughts with the two blondes and began to feel she had finally found herself again.

A couple of times she hinted to Den that she would rather

live here permanently than with Anna, but Den was non-committal. She learnt that the two blondes had a flat of their own, for all that they seemed to be around here twenty-four hours a day. So maybe it would be cooler to keep her lodgings separate. It would not do to become too dependent.

One afternoon the two blondes took her out to the suburbs to see the band they belonged to. They had an old stone barn at the end of an overgrown path, surrounded by brambles, nettles and shrubs, overlooked somehow when the houses had moved this way.

There was no electricity in the barn, but that was of no importance as they turned out to be wholly acoustic, running the gamut from saxophone to glockenspiel, from upright piano to crashing cymbals. They made a chaotic cacophonic clash of rhythms, and Carrie was entranced.

'What do you think?' they beamed, quite able to see what she had thought.

'Brilliant,' she breathed, asking if they had played anywhere much.

'Just a couple of places,' said the silvery blonde, whose name was Toni. 'We're not really good enough yet.'

Carrie thought they were a thousand times better than Den's band.

'No one wants to hear this sort of music,' said the orangey blonde, whose name was Candi. 'Not up here, anyway.'

'You should do some tapes,' suggested Carrie, thinking of John Peel.

The two blondes grimaced rather hopelessly, but they were clearly well-pleased at being so praised, praise being precisely what they lived for most.

'Carrie says we're far better than you lot,' Toni announced when they returned to the basement, waltzing into the bass player's bedroom-cum-communal TV room.

Carrie grinned, easing into the room behind the imperial duo, and discovered Den with his arm protectively around the shoulders of some redhead, his other hand gently touching her lips.

No one so much as glanced at her to see how she took it, this being Den's normal pattern of rotating women and no more than anyone had expected. She sat down jerkily, anger rising with the hurt, and stared at the TV screen. It occurred to her that if she had moved out of Anna's flat she would now be homeless. It occurred to her that far from having found a new centre of gravity at which to secure herself she was suddenly completely without the major reason for being accepted around here at all. It occurred to her that it would have been better to have been a little more clear-headed instead of being so intent upon turning herself into a mere groupie.

With crimsoned embarrassment she recalled how she had poured her soul out to Den every night. Like an untutored adolescent hoping to exchange confidences for security. She shrank back against the wall, glad that they were looking at the TV and not at her.

Slowly, insanely slowly to Carrie, people began to take in that there was a potentially distressing scenario here, and they began to dart quick glances at her. The two blondes were trading significant looks, and the singer paid unusually close attention to her expression when he directed some casual comment at her. Den and the singer were particularly tight together. Carrie dared not imagine how much of her nightly torments Den had passed on to him.

As the TV programme rolled by, one set of commercials succeeding another, she knew she was approaching what could only be a humiliating crisis: whether to stay here and have everyone watch her as Den and this other girl went off to bed together; or whether to get up and go, surrender her right to sleep in the house at all, quietly slip back to being an outsider, one of the crowd, as alone as ever.

Den said to her, unexpectedly, 'So you like Toni's band better than us, eh?'

All eyes swivelled in her direction.

'Yeh,' she said. 'I think they're great.' It sounded ingratiating and insulting both at once. The two blondes were suddenly very still, not wanting to be dragged in as pawns.

Carrie expected the assault to be followed up, but Den seemed to have nothing more to say about it.

'Anyway,' she announced, standing up. 'I've got to be going. I've got a friend coming up from London tonight, he'll be here by the time I get home.'

Several people stood to express their regrets at her leaving and to wish her goodbye, so great was their relief.

She could almost believe they were genuinely sorry to see her go.

Anna did not know what to make of Carrie by this time. No civility or kindness seemed to reach her, casually ignoring her seemed as welcome to her as thoughtful attention, she often hid in her room as if she could not even bear to be thought of. Yet at other times she would sit obstinately in the way, for she was now at home much more often, almost demanding to be spoken to, yet sullen and impervious. It was as though, whatever it was she truly wanted, she herself had no idea what it was or even if, should it be offered, she would actually accept it. Anna began to think of ways of throwing her out and finding herself a more congenial flatmate.

Things were little better at the band's place. Den had expected her to quietly disappear, which is what girls usually did in such circumstances, and her continued presence there as if she belonged in some way quite separate to his attentions was very disconcerting.

Her manner initially was perfectly cheerful, apparently quite undaunted by his rejection of her. But he had a keen enough eye for her that he was able to pick out the insecurity hiding just underneath, and he worked at that steadily when she was not around.

'Did she really live in London?' he might say if her name came up. 'I know what she says, but she doesn't sound like it, really, when you listen to her voice. She can't have been there long.'

'A day or two,' grinned the singer. 'Went down for the weekend once.'

And because Den undeniably knew her better than anyone, the next time Carrie came around people seemed to be listening to her with peculiar attention, and if she chanced to mention London they would get a peculiar look in their eyes and forget to answer her.

'Actually, I think Carrie was still a virgin,' Den would say, popping it into general conversation. 'I know she doesn't look it, but she's had plenty of years to work up an act.'

They became off-hand, they stopped listening to her halfway

through what she had to say. Her cheerfulness became ever more mournful.

'What's wrong with her these days?' the silvery blonde asked the other, in all honesty. 'She looks like she gets whipped every morning before breakfast.'

'I wish someone would whip me every morning before breakfast,' the other replied, lasciviously.

'How's the band?' Carrie asked when she saw them a little later.

'Great,' they said.

'Shall I come round and hear you practise?' How could it sound so feeble and imploring? It was such a simple, casual suggestion. She felt as if she had just asked them to please love her for she had no one else. She looked so crushed when they turned away, not knowing any more how to cope with her. Pretty soon they too began to giggle at her.

One afternoon Carrie was leafing through a magazine while Den was sitting doodling in the margins of a music paper, the two blondes watching him and making caustic comments.

'Who's that?' he said finally, sketching something grotesque yet somehow familiar. They didn't know. It resembled if anything a drowned cat in a Toyah costume.

Den lowered his voice, just loud enough for her to hear.

'Carrie,' he whispered, and the twosome exploded helplessly, half ashamed but half delighted.

Carrie pretended not to notice. Twenty minutes later she left, never to come back.

Den watched her go.

She really was quite cuddly. Maybe he should start being nice to her again.

So now she was on Anna's hands all hours of the day, leaving the flat only to mope about the streets. It seemed there was nothing left in her life worth bothering about. She no longer had any of her old props to fall back on. No friends (what friends?), no drugs (big deal), not even music. Music just reminded her of all the scars she had so suddenly accumulated. Besides, everything sounded the same these days, all the old excitement, all the sense of challenge and danger, had completely vanished.

She had never known a time when there had been so literally nothing. Even during her last months in London she had had *something,* even if only a chafing hope of things eventually getting better.

Anna saw her one day walking along the city wall, paying no attention to the view, just mechanically putting one foot down after another.

Anna had certainly not failed to notice Carrie's earlier disdain. She had taken her present moodiness to be in large part a simple extension of it. Now, however, she began to suspect that she herself was in fact neither source nor target, and possibly something much deeper was troubling Carrie. She felt some quiet pity, wondered if there was some way Carrie could be touched and comforted.

Sometimes she felt so shell-like. She doubted that she had any real comfort left inside her to give.

She decided she would make one final effort to break through to Carrie, and if nothing came of it she would throw her out. Her own life, after all, was not exactly roses and kisses.

Anna and Carrie sat over the kitchen table, nursing cups of coffee. Anna made most of the conversation, watching Carrie all the while, noticing the changes that recent days had made in her which suggested that she too wanted a closer link between them. Carrie, indeed, was all too well aware of how dismissive she had been of Anna, and now that Anna seemed to be the only companion she had left her earlier aloofness was something she did not like to recall.

Anna suggested they go into the lounge. She took the coffee pot while Carrie followed with the cups. She had to find out what had been going on. Carrie acted evasively bored, but when pressed gave a tired, dry rundown of the previous few weeks.

'People get involved in their own lives,' Anna said, trying to make Carrie feel less a victim of casual malice. 'The busier you are, the less easy it is to make sense of someone who doesn't fit.'

She saw her wince at that. Carrie, she realised, was accustomed to choosing where she would or would not fit.

Carrie got up, and to give herself purpose flipped idly through

Anna's records. There was a lot of sixties stuff, some of it quite adventurous, not just the usual memorabilia. After that it tailed off into softer, blander material, much of it American, all very predictable. She wandered over to the bookshelf, fingering through the books.

'I don't know how you can read things like this,' she said, looking through then putting back a thick hardback on the Christian Fathers.

'It's quite fascinating once you get into it.'

'I could never get into stuff like that.'

She sat down again, up close to the electric fire. The little room felt pleasant now, warm and friendly. Sometimes, when she was alone, the flat felt tomb-like. It occurred to her that she had not once seen a third person here. Carrie had always had someone or other around. She wondered how Anna stood it.

'Tell me about Swank,' Anna said, having heard no more than brief mention of his name, but judging that there was more to be told.

'Oh,' said Carrie. 'I dunno . . . you roll a ball down a hill and it goes great till it reaches the valley bottom, it even rolls up the other side a little. But then it rolls back and gets stuck.'

She summarised the lengthy and sometimes convoluted story of her dealings with Swank.

'He left me,' was all she said in conclusion. That and, 'It was my fault. No wonder he left me, the way I was acting.'

'Do you want him back?'

Carrie sighed. 'Thing is,' she said, 'how do you have a permanent relationship that isn't just a marriage without vows?'

And then, 'If we had been married he couldn't have just left me like that. He would have had to stay and help me sort myself out.'

She did not like feeling so miserable over Swank. She was not accustomed to thinking of herself as someone so vulnerable.

'We don't get what we want, we get what we need,' Anna said softly, as if repeating a formula.

'Bollocks,' muttered Carrie.

'We get in touch as best we can with whatever deity it is that fits us, and we try to hear what he has to say and try to shape our lives so that we co-operate instead of working at cross-purposes. So little of it is ultimately up to us, anyway. So you accept what the greater powers have in store for you and work with them and shorten the odds.'

'And you believe all that?'

'Yes.' She said it as if she had been simply asserting the principle of heliocentricity.

'Yeh, well I've done a bit of thinking about God in my time,' said Carrie bitterly. 'I'll tell you what God is all about. It's like when they say he sees every sparrow that falls. All right, so he sees. But he doesn't do anything about it, does he? He still lets it happen. Fucking sparrow's starved to death or shot or something, it doesn't do him any good if God's standing watching it all. Maybe the sparrow didn't want to starve or be shot, but that's obviously exactly what he needed!'

'You shouldn't fight things so much.'

'I always fight things,' said Carrie. 'When I can't fight I get miserable.'

'The longer you fight the more embittered you get and the less able to salvage anything. Endless fighting is like a poison. The anger accumulates and eventually destroys you.'

Carrie thought of her constant fighting with Swank. Mostly they had good honest fights, they half killed each other and then they both forgot it and were sweeter to each other than ever. Fighting brought them together as much as anything. Only, later . . .

But then, later they had not really been fighting. She had been moaning, constantly trying to explain her unhappiness to him. He had been fed up. A good knock-down fight might have put everything on the right track again.

'Maybe,' she said. There were other kinds of fighting. They had not done her much good.

'Don't you ever get lonely here?' she asked. 'Aren't you afraid of spending your whole life here?'

She was not looking at Anna when she said this, and so missed the fleeting despair that crossed her face.

'I get by,' Anna replied. She let her eyes wander over the bars of the fire, wondering if she dared say something that seemed embarrassingly childish.

'It's sort of like Beauty and the Beast. I think you've got to be emotionally well fed to be able to go beyond yourself and look beneath the surface of someone else, into the heart of the beast, so to speak. Many people run on half empty so much of the time, they've barely got enough love for themselves. So beasts go around being ever more beastly just out of self-protection. I suppose me and my beast just haven't recognised each other.'

Or more likely, I am the beast and there are no beauties.

To Carrie this seemed strangely wise. She and Swank fought like beasts, they loved like beasts, they tumbled around together like beasts. Big, furry, catlike beasts. Only when circumstances had drained her so she was running on empty did the catlike creature in her become unable to reach out to the same creature in Swank, and Swank turned away from her in disappointed disgust, with all the proper surliness of the true beast.

There was to Carrie something very wondrous in the way Anna had been able to cut through things as effectively as that, to put her finger on such an essential point, all on the basis of the bare details that Carrie had told her. She looked at Anna with new eyes, discarding what she had seen before, seeing now something very special.

'I think that's very true,' she said.

'All those old stories have a lot of truth in them,' Anna said, vaguely, relieved she had not been laughed at.

In that moment Carrie came to greatly admire Anna. Anna seemed to have the depth, the maturity, to see the world as it was, a faculty Carrie had never before appreciated. Maturity to Carrie had always meant a desolate solidity, a surrender of autonomy. That maturity could mean wisdom, rising Goddess-like above all else, seeing the underlying truth of things, was not something that had ever occurred to her.

What did it matter if, *for now*, Anna lived alone in her flat? Anna could clearly see the truth of the case, that there were times to pull yourself in, to wait upon events, to try and make sense of everything, to grow and re-assess before moving out into the world again. She had made a fool of herself with Den and his friends. Anna, she believed, would have had the awareness not to do that. Wisdom and maturity now became unexpectedly precious commodities, and she wanted them more than anything else.

In truth she was far more experienced than Anna in most of

the ways of the world. But her experiences seemed to have boxed her in, left her running around bull-headed and finally exhausted. What she saw in Anna seemed to soothe and offer new growth.

Anna poured herself some more coffee and relaxed back into the chair, glad they were finally having a decent conversation. She had not really wanted to go through all the trauma of seeking someone to share her flat again, and now it seemed as if things could probably work out all right. It just needed a little attention and a little sympathy.

It is so hard to keep your soul in one piece, you need someone there as a mirror, someone there to give when you need to take. You bind your soul together and the better you bind it the more people are impressed by your self-control and your ability to get along without them. Or else you don't bind it tightly enough, you fall apart, and they shy skittishly away.

'I've got a couple of weeks' holiday starting on Saturday,' she said. 'Why not help me get re-acquainted with the city?'

Actually they spent very little time on acquainting or re-acquainting themselves with the city. They did spend a day or two on the tourist spots, but mostly they just lived the life of the idle, shopping without doing too much buying, and being fairly extravagant about where they went for lunch. Carrie began to shrug off some of her recent discontent, allowing herself to be warmed by the ancient rubbed-in humanity of the city's streets and by the modern bustle that in such a setting kept slipping obstinately back in time and mingling indistinguishably with its ancestors.

There was a feeling in those streets that only forms changed, humanity remained eternal: always hurrying about, always intent on the business at hand, yet always with time for a contemplative snack, a crude joke, an offering of kindness. These noisy streets seemed more timeless than even the ancient cathedral, for the mere forms seemed to have left the cathedral behind.

They talked as well as looked. They talked of everything in those two weeks. They talked as Carrie had never talked to anyone before.

She was interested by Anna's claims to religious faith. Her

own attitude to religion had been shaped by school and the measured tones of Radio Four, a combination of All Things Bright And Beautiful and something very earnest and rather desiccated. By the books in the flat she had assumed that Anna was basically a Christian, although with some curious side interests. But Anna replied that she was not a Christian at all.

'What then?' Carrie asked, thinking, Jew? Buddhist?

'Pagan, actually,' Anna admitted.

Carrie thought of bearded hippies frolicking in the woodlands and being worthy about nuclear power and animal liberation, dining on magic mushrooms and searching for fairy-folk beneath the hedgerows. That or ancient Jupiter having it off with all the local girls and youths. It took Anna right out of the company of museum attendants, where Christianity seemed to place her, and put her into the class of lighthouse-keepers and historians of underwear.

'That's weird,' was all she could think of in reply.

But Anna said paganism was not at all like that. It mostly meant simply accepting that God appears to people in many different ways, and in the plural as well as the singular.

'I did go to church once, about eight years ago,' Carrie said. 'There didn't seem a lot of point to it.'

'I never find anything in churches either,' said Anna. 'Except when they're empty. But I'm not a pagan because I have any great complaint against the churches or even Christianity. They could alter the churches around any way they liked, I'd still be a pagan because paganism feels right to me while Christianity doesn't.'

They were walking along a street of little shops as they discussed this. Carrie thought it extremely odd to be calmly talking about God amidst traffic and shoppers and the trickle of drizzle, with the day's newspapers displayed on the rack outside the newsagents.

Back in the flat, with the door closed and evening descending, she felt less inhibited about it and probed deeper, intrigued.

'First,' began Anna, settling down for a long siege, 'there is a Deity, the Creator, who is naturally of neither sex but it's simpler, just by convention, to say "he". This Deity is external to the universe, yet woven into its very fabric. Just as Beethoven was the external creator of his music yet is personally present in every note wherever it is performed.'

'Why does there have to be a Creator?' Carrie asked.

'Well logically there doesn't. There's no real reason why the universe shouldn't go on expanding and contracting, appearing and vanishing, for eternity in both directions. But religion seems to put you in touch with something universal, all-embracing, and people tend to identify that something with the force behind the universe. But it is curious that the laws governing the universe and the way matter is formed and shapes itself rest upon a knife-edge, and only very slight differences in those laws would have made the very existence of life impossible. Or so I gather from my reading. Those natural laws are like the thoughts of God, who brings everything into existence by his own will, the word made flesh.

'But that's just rational speculation. Most people don't believe in God because they've rationally proved some probability of there being one. Instead the Deity presents itself to us in a way that we can directly perceive. Sometimes we're encouraged to look deep within ourselves and we find the Deity at the centre of our deepest essence, just as he is present in the deepest essence of all the rest of the universe. Or sometimes the Deity comes upon us from outside and overwhelms us in a way we never forget.'

'That happened to me!' Carrie said, suddenly making sense of the strange thing that had happened to her one day in the bath. She described it to Anna in vivid detail. 'I thought I was going mad.'

'Something such as that,' Anna said, 'even if it only happens once in your entire life, makes atheism seem like a blind man criticising art. To me an atheist is almost by definition someone who has never had such an experience.'

Carrie was impressed. To have had an overwhelming experience of God's immediate presence made her feel rather saint-like. She wondered how Swank would react if she told him she had been specially called apart by God himself. Kill himself laughing, probably.

'So why be a pagan if God is universal and appears to everyone? Why not just be a Christian or something?'

'Different cultures need different gods, and so do different people. It's like light shining through a prism. Everyone has a part of the religious spectrum that to them feels exactly right.

We're all shaped by the world we live in, so mostly we feel happiest with the forms that are accepted by everyone around us. But sometimes we don't, and then we have to be free to find the form that fits us best. For me, it's paganism.'

Carrie felt dissatisfied with this. It was clear that Anna was still holding something back.

'You mean like Apollo? Venus?'

Anna had a lot of problems in her life. She was no saint. She was not even particularly happy much of the time. She was the last person to claim to be a guru or a mystic. How to explain the glow at the centre of her heart that helped her hold herself up when times got exceptionally rough, and added a special violet-tinged delight when times were good? How to explain that she called this glow by one name and not by another, and gave it one face and not another, and that both name and face seemed to have been suggested to her by the glow itself?

She said, picking her words, 'To me the Deity is ultimately not God but Goddess. I've read things about her that make sense because they seem to agree with what I myself have felt. I think of her as the Triple Goddess, maid, mother and crone, because that is the ancient form given to her but also because that identifies her intimately with all phases of life. She incorporates in her evil and death just as much as good and life, because those things are part of the world and the world is her creation. Seeing those things as part of the divine wholeness makes them rather easier to bear. As for names . . . Isis, Athene, Cerridwen, Ishtar, Kali. Even Mary is just the Goddess in human form. She has many names. You can fit together the names and the elements of her triple aspects almost endlessly to express that particular understanding of her that you most need to make clear at any one time. Mostly I call her Isis. It's an old name, and it's a name I like.'

As Anna spoke all this, Carrie saw that something eternal came into her face, some wise, ageless beauty, as if for those moments Anna herself was illuminated by the touch of her Goddess. But the source of it was Anna too, some sense that she had come to an understanding with the world and its Deity, that they knew each other pretty well, that she had survived rough patches with something precious not only intact but actually stronger.

Was Anna's Goddess, Carrie wondered, somehow a result of

her own essential self, or was her own particular self brought to some essential wholeness by her Goddess?

'I don't even know what questions to ask,' Carrie said, yet anxious to know more.

'That's why they say faith means trust,' Anna went on, not hearing. 'You can trust something like that, something real and personal. You can wholly believe that, ultimately, it has your own best interests at heart.'

That prompted for Carrie other, more disturbing ideas. 'What about starving children?' she asked. What about me? thinking that her own life was not exactly an example of benign, divine concern.

Anna shook her head. 'The simple, glib answer is that people are born over and over again and sometimes are here with specific lessons to learn through specific experiences, and further that within that framework we have free will to make as much of a foul-up as we are capable of. I find you can't really make sense of your troubles until they're over, and even then it's your own sufferings that make sense, not those of the whole world. Whether or not I could accept that if I was starving I don't know. I just have to have faith that the Goddess works things out for the people of Africa or Bangladesh in the same way that she works things out for me. I'm not aware that famines produce great crops of atheists.'

It was a novel way of looking at things for Carrie. She did not know if she believed it all. But she thought she would hold on to it for a while, just in case.

'I can't take any more of this,' she said. 'Not for tonight.'

'Shall we go to see a film?' Anna suggested. It had been quite some time since she had had someone to go to the cinema with. Things, she hoped, were looking up.

They talked about other things too, of course. They talked about politics. Carrie said, 'When your relatives tell you you're not welcome in their homes and when they get off on fantasising all sorts of perversions then accuse you of doing them, you start to support everything that they're afraid of and against. Or when I was on the game, the way the Bill used to leer, and they always used to think they could give you shit because you had no protection against them. It doesn't exactly make you a law-and-order Conservative. Or when you get some dried-up, clapped-out, old hag scowling at you in the street because you've got spiky hair, there's times when there's nothing I wouldn't do to get back at people like that.'

Hearing this, Anna thought she understood the anger that she sometimes saw well up in Carrie. It seemed to be quite beyond her own volition, quite separate from any circumstances, great black globules of it that she had to physically push back. It was as if she had been fighting for so long, against enemies both real and illusory, that the anger had gained a life and will of its own. Normally she would have found a target somewhere in the front of her mind and attributed the anger to that. Now there was no target ready at hand and her fury confused and alarmed her.

Anna decided she would teach her some of the simple meditation techniques she knew. She sat Carrie down one evening, cross-legged on the rug, taught her to breathe in certain ways and explained why, and taught her how to visualise the primary colours to stir up psychic energies.

But she did not want to ignore the miraculous, or at least the impression of it, for the miraculous was what would most capture the imagination. Years before, as a child, she had sent away to a comic for a Pony Club badge. The comics had long since been thrown out, but the badge she had kept for its nostalgic associations. She folded it in paper to disguise it, put it in an envelope, and gave the envelope to Carrie, telling her to say what was in it.

'Don't worry about looking at it,' she said, as Carrie tried to discover the contents through sight and touch. 'Hold it in your palms and close your eyes. Look inside yourself, that's where the answer is.'

But Carrie could make nothing of it.

'What do you see in your mind?' Anna persisted. 'What images are in your head, right at this moment?'

'I keep thinking of school,' said Carrie, hopelessly, and she could see in her imagination a concrete playground, not one she recognised, and young girls in winter clothing.

'So what age do you think I was when I got that object?' Anna asked, softly.

Carrie caught on in a sudden rush of intuition. She let her imagination run free and called out whatever she saw. 'Horses,' she said. 'By themselves. In a field.'

'I loved horses,' said Anna. 'I always wanted one.'

'A black disc on a pale background. With coloured markings on it. I can't make them out. Some kind of drawing.'

Anna let her open the envelope.

'I didn't think it was as easy as that,' Carrie said, rather shaken, looking at the round black badge with its painting of a girl and a horse's head.

'Well it is easy, so don't go thinking you're anything special,' Anna warned. But secretly she was proud.

'I thought there were supposed to be secret mantras and things?'

'Do you want a mantra?' Anna asked, lightly. 'There are people who would charge you a fortune for a phoney mantra.' She taught her Om Mani Padme Hum, how to say it, how to spell it so she would remember it more clearly, and how to breathe as she repeated it.

'Does it mean anything?' Carrie asked.

'Om you can think of as the Deity, reality, the underlying principle of everything. Hum is like a challenge to the more wooden materialistic parts of your mind. Mani Padme means the Jewel in the Lotus. The lotus is the material world, the jewel is the glow of something hidden inside it. Do you understand? It's one of those things that has to come from yourself before you can really comprehend it.'

Carrie repeated it cautiously. How strange that Anna, a normal person in a normal flat above a shop, should know all these bizarre things. Her thoughts were suddenly cast back to Swank, somewhere in London. What was she doing sitting here? She still did not really know, but as yet she had no plans to leave.

There was a lot of time for thinking, as well. Sometimes when she and Anna sat quietly, with the clock and the silence uniting them in separate tranquillities. Sometimes alone in her room, looking out of her window over the roofs. Roofs were such functional things, their drab, grey slates added that extra touch of permanency to the houses beneath. Yet there was also something very romantic about them. In *Mary Poppins*, Carrie had found the dancing on the rooftops even more magical than the popping into pavement pictures. How old had she been when she saw *Mary Poppins*?

Thinking of roofs and what goes on beneath them, she

thought of the nut in its shell, the life in the seed, the milk in the bottle, the water in the tap. How electricity flows through a dead construction of plastic and metal and calls it into life and movement.

She thought of the raw rowdy songs of half-a-dozen years ago, how they were nothing but noise to most people, yet for her they rang with strong emotions that were already ringing aloud inside her. How the guitar, rhythm without tune, fast, rough-edged, preferably slightly awry from the beat, could impact upon something physical inside you that was its exact counterpart, and provoke a rush of energy and even chaos.

Other pictures appeared in her mind, unbidden. In all the diversity of the natural world there was the unity of life and the development of life. In the diversity of the physical there was the common unity of matter itself and the strict limits imposed on the way matter could shape itself into objects and beings. In the complexity of the universe was the unifying substructure of mathematics, the thoughts of God as Anna put it, a concept wholly alien to Carrie until now. She thought of a picture she had seen of a black hole, with the lines that represented the shape of the universe dipping into the funnel. This matrix, this conceptual structure, underlay all that was and caused it to have form.

In the human mind, amidst the jumble of everyday concerns and long-term anxieties, disguised by all that had been taught, learnt, and unlearnt, was the Self. Finding that Selfhood, extracting it from all the clutter, gave order to understanding and focus to action. Going to the world first without reaching down to the Self simply built up the clutter and arranged it in rigid patterns that were hard to break.

But because the jewel is hidden in the lotus you cannot find the jewel if you ignore its cradle, life. She had never before connected the two and so her impression of the jewel had always been of something fantastical and extraneous. By looking as best she could at life and the Self she saw the jewel hidden in both, and saw in it the same matrix that bound together the Universe, the same thing that Anna called the Goddess, a something special that somewhere inside her evoked an intensely welcoming response.

She was pleased with herself for having worked this out. She did not know if it was all true, but it made an intuitive sort of sense. She could at least rely on it until she confirmed it or until she came up with something better.

Anna also had been doing some thinking.

She had become used to not noticing herself in mirrors on a morning, no more at least than was needed to be sure she was arranged in some reasonable order without unsightly smudges or prominent discontinuities. Now she stood there taking a good close look. She did not like it. She looked at her face and her clothes, seeing herself wrongly for the most part, in bits and pieces, focusing on the elements that proved she was no longer as young as Carrie, missing the wholeness altogether.

There were her clothes in particular. They were quite stylish, but the style would be thought more durable than exciting. Well, she thought, she could not take care of them just like that. She had no confidence in her ability to all at once update her entire wardrobe without making herself look ridiculous. It would have to be done bit by bit. But updated it must certainly be.

Perhaps by updating the externals to correspond with the enlivening influence of Carrie and the confidence inspired by a renewed interest in daily life, perhaps she could shake herself out of the neat little run-around she had cornered herself into.

She flicked her hair with a grimace. There was something else that needed updating. The kids on the street, the women on television, the models on the hair fashion pages, they cut it, shaped it, coloured it, used their imaginations on it. She wrapped a lock around her finger and tugged absently, feeling the familiar pressure on her scalp. It made her think of how much fuss it was washing and brushing and generally looking after such an unwieldy mass of useless hair.

Well, she would start there. She could get that taken care of in a morning. As for the clothes, she would keep an eye open, there were boutiques and markets, she could put something worthwhile together, and then just see . . .

So when Carrie came home one afternoon from a walk by the river she found a blonde adolescent sitting at the kitchen table drinking Coke from a can and reading a trashy novel about the very rich.

This startling vision looked up, grinning gleefully, and it was Anna.

Carrie stared, appalled. Then she assumed nonchalance and tried to pretend she had not even noticed. But all through the evening she kept looking, trying to see the old Anna in the new. It was still the same face, even more so now that you saw it whole and unadorned. It was still the same voice, calm, self-controlled, warm at times but edged with something rather severe. The likeness was close enough for Carrie to keep up the pretence and avoid disturbing the comfortable ebb and flow they had settled into.

But none the less, she was appalled.

Later, alone, segments of their conversations would return to her, as they do, and she could not help clothing Anna's image in the wonderful mass of hair that had suddenly gone. In her mind's eye she saw how Anna's expressions had only needed their accustomed framing, the dark emphasis that the hair gave to the eyes, to make the stranger of this afternoon back into the friend she had come to feel so trusting of.

Yet this was absurd, selfish even. What really appalled her was not the deed itself but what it had suddenly revealed. For Anna, whom she had thought so beautiful and such an embodiment of wisdom and self-acceptance, had thus declared herself to be as flighty and as unsure of herself as anyone else, anxious for her lost youth, unsure of her own worth, afraid of growing old. Anna was no better than everyone else, dissatisfied, for ever trying to circle backwards in order to go forwards, trying to rely on frills and spices to cover a lack of substance.

It was the same old treadmill. Carrie had two visions of herself at thirty-five. One was the anonymous housewife sinking unresisting into gentle oblivion. The other was an older version of her present self, seeking out noise and youth as an antidote to deterioration, endlessly repeating her experiences with Den and coming to accept it as normal, ever more out of touch, ever more ignored, a slow decay into desolation.

In Anna she thought she had found an alternative to this. She had thought Anna such a pool of profound depths, had seen in her the possibility of a rising above and a moving beyond, a re-creation not in the usual pattern of butterfly to moth, but from wren or starling to raven or owl.

She felt appalled.

Over the next couple of days Anna noticed a new flippancy in Carrie, a new twist in her cavalcade of emotional masks. There was a new willingness to make jokes of everything, a reluctance to return to the heavy discussions of the past two weeks. She took it as a sign of Carrie's growing recovery, felt able to have new confidence in their friendship, not be quite the wise instructress she had been before. It did not occur to her that Carrie was simply not so in awe of her any more. It had never occurred to her that Carrie was in awe of her in the first place, and she never would have wanted it.

Anna resumed her work, and Carrie spent her days in secret musings. She said once, when Anna came home, 'I suppose its different for people who get married. They have to jump from irresponsible youth to citizen and provider almost in one day.'

She had been wondering about herself and Swank. She could not imagine Swank married. If she went back and sought out Swank would he want her? Or would she find him contentedly shacked up with someone else? Suppose he wanted her back and suppose she persuaded him to marry her, would it help move her on to some new phase of being – as she so desperately wanted – or would it simply trap her in the exercise-wheel existence that so many others were happily caught in? She could hardly even begin to see the answers.

Anna seemed to have very little to say about these new problems. Carrie was beginning to notice that there were things Anna did not like to talk about, particularly personal things, things that related to past love affairs and their desecrations. Now that the first cracks had been made, she was coming to see that Anna did not have her past as well worked out or as serenely come to terms with as it had appeared. She still bore the tranquillised consequences of old hurts that had ripped out whole chunks of her.

She should, by rights, in the name of friendship, do some subtle probing to help Anna bring these wounds out into private view where perhaps they could be soothed or even found to be fully healed. But she shrank from it. It was like being asked to cure your dentist's toothache.

They went to the weekend flea market and Carrie watched

in silent fascination as Anna's wardrobe underwent a dramatic cultural revolution. Carrie had spent two weeks trying to drag herself up to Anna's heights, and now here was Anna determined to re-occupy the uncertain plains Carrie had been so anxious to abandon. By now Carrie had a pretty good idea of what was going on, but that made it no easier to accept.

Anna began to be aware that Carrie was withdrawing herself. Not into disdain or depression, like before. Just withdrawing.

'Do you get bored here alone all day?' she asked, suspecting that to be the cause.

'I do a bit,' said Carrie, not answering.

'Maybe you could get a job somewhere?'

Why not get a job? Assuming a job could be got. Anna had a job she liked, other people had jobs they liked, why should she not discover a job she liked?

Maybe in London she could find a job. Or find Swank.

Maybe Swank was different now, just like she was, going through changes just like her. Maybe she could nudge him along, maybe he would be able to nudge her along.

Imagine Swank as a responsible citizen.

Or rather, better, just imagine Swank.

They would be more sensible about things. Not endlessly rushing after things, not wasting energy on scowling at everyone just because the world didn't suit them.

She didn't need a job. They could get by on the dole. Not for ever, perhaps, but for long enough. What she needed was activity and familiar company, Swank's irascibility and Swank's waywardness. This place was like a tomb. Swank had always lead from the front while she had guided from the sides. She had things to show him now, she could do some of the leading.

They always did good together, her and Swank.

Anna felt depressed at Carrie's abrupt departure. But she knew she should have expected it. Carrie had her own life, after all, there was nothing to hold her here when there were friends of her own elsewhere. She had been foolish to even hope for it.

Anna stopped dyeing her hair and let it grow again.

Later she got a very good job in local radio and married a producer.